THE KINGFISHER BOOK OF
CLASSIC
CHRISTMAS
STORIES

For Suzannah and Lucy, with love—I. W.

KINGFISHER
a Houghton Mifflin Company imprint
222 Berkeley Street
Boston, Massachusetts 02116
www.houghtonmifflinbooks.com
First published in 2004
2 4 6 8 10 9 7 5 3 1

LIBRARY OF CONGRESS CATALOGING-IN-PUBLICATION DATA
The Kingfisher book of classic Christmas stories / chosen by Ian Whybrow.
p. cm.
Summary: An anthology of fourteen Christmas stories, both previously published and newly commissioned, by such
authors as Louisa May Alcott and William Dean Howells, and illustrated by such artists as Anna C. Leplar and Paolo D'Altan.
ISBN 0-7534-5732-6
1. Christmas—Juvenile fiction. 2. Children's stories, American. [1. Christmas—Fiction. 2. Short stories.] I. Whybrow, Ian.
PZ5.K57557 2004
[Fic]—dc22   2004007504

Printed in China
1TR/0804/PROSP/FR(FR)/157MA

THE KINGFISHER BOOK OF CLASSIC CHRISTMAS STORIES

Selected by Ian Whybrow

KINGFISHER

BOSTON

Contents

Foreword

A tangerine in the toe with at least three seeds in every segment; a handful of mixed nuts in the heel . . . They were there, definitely . . . but what else was in my Christmas stocking when I was a boy? Ah, yes!—a tin box of watercolors from Woolworth's containing a paintbrush and two oblong dents for mixing all the colors together until they became brown. Then there was a printing set with little rubber letters, an ink pad, and a pair of tweezers for pinching your sisters' bottoms. I remember a pale blue soap policeman, a Christmas cracker that stung your knuckles when it popped, a clockwork mouse . . .

Isn't it fascinating that Christmas presents tell you so much—about the giver as well as the receiver? The contents of my stocking are a far cry from what children get for Christmas today—but they were a real treat to me in the 1950s when there wasn't much money around. In this collection there are plenty of opportunities to find out about Christmas giving around the world, from humble weeds in a traditional Mexican story to a gift of handmade shoes in a French folktale.

No candy in my stocking, notice. They were still "on the ration" then, so they had to be carefully wrapped and placed on the pile of packages at the far end of my bed, because packages were for special stuff like comic books and building sets and windup train sets and cowboy outfits. Yee-haah for the five-gallon felt hat, the chaps, cap pistol, holster, and shiny sheriff's badge! Once I even got an enormous chocolate bar, all bumpy with bits in it. I suspected it was for sharing and pigged out on the whole thing before my sisters even laid eyes on it.

I was obsessed with food, especially candy, so it's not really surprising that I've chosen plenty of stories to make your mouth water. The Cratchits' feast from Charles Dickens' *A Christmas Carol* is here, of course, along with homemade delights in L. M. Montgomery's story, *Aunt Cyrilla's Christmas Basket* and the improvised spread in Kenneth Grahame's *Christmas at Mole End*.

My Christmas day always passed by in a blur. Roast chicken—a once-a-year-treat—for dinner. A scattering of snow, if you were lucky. Never enough. Singing "Silent Night" at the top of my lungs in the choir at St. Saviour's. Quarreling with my cousins, while Dad and Uncle Jack were cloistered in the sitting room for hours building a towering crane made from my building set. When I proudly demolished it with my little wrench in no time at all after dinner, I was astonished to be roared at rather than congratulated for my brilliance. So visitors, squabbles, and misunderstandings we have aplenty in stories such as *The Nutcracker*, *Befana and the Three Wise Men*, and *A Very Big Cat*.

Christmas for me as a boy was divided into periods of yearning, overexcitement, overindulgence, and finally of mourning for vital parts of presents that mysteriously disappeared five minutes after being unwrapped. My jigsaw puzzle always had a piece of sky missing, my paintbrush immediately rolled down a crack between the floorboards, and anything clockwork died of overwinding.

Christmas was all about the gifts I received—I don't remember thoughts of giving.

I've tried to make up for my shortcomings in this collection with plenty of stories full of a more generous, true Christmas spirit, where the focus is on the welfare of others. Many come from the 1800s and the first half of the 1900s, during which time the traditional patterns for our modern festive season were laid down. As well as including plenty of old favorites, I've chosen some less well-known folktales and Yuletide legends.

I've always loved reading stories aloud and being read to, so I've tried to get together a well-written and entertaining mixture that the whole family can grow up with, ponder, and discuss. It's one that readers of every age group can treasure and revisit again and again—sometimes alone, sometimes with other people. Younger members of the family will enjoy *Becky's Christmas Dream* and *The Elves and the Shoemaker*. Other stories, such as the extracts from *A Christmas Carol* and *The Wind in the Willows*, are richer in their language and ideas, so that they will appeal to older children. I hope every reader will find something in this collection to fill them with the Christmas spirit.

Merry Christmas, everyone—and happy reading!

The First Christmas

ANNE ADENEY

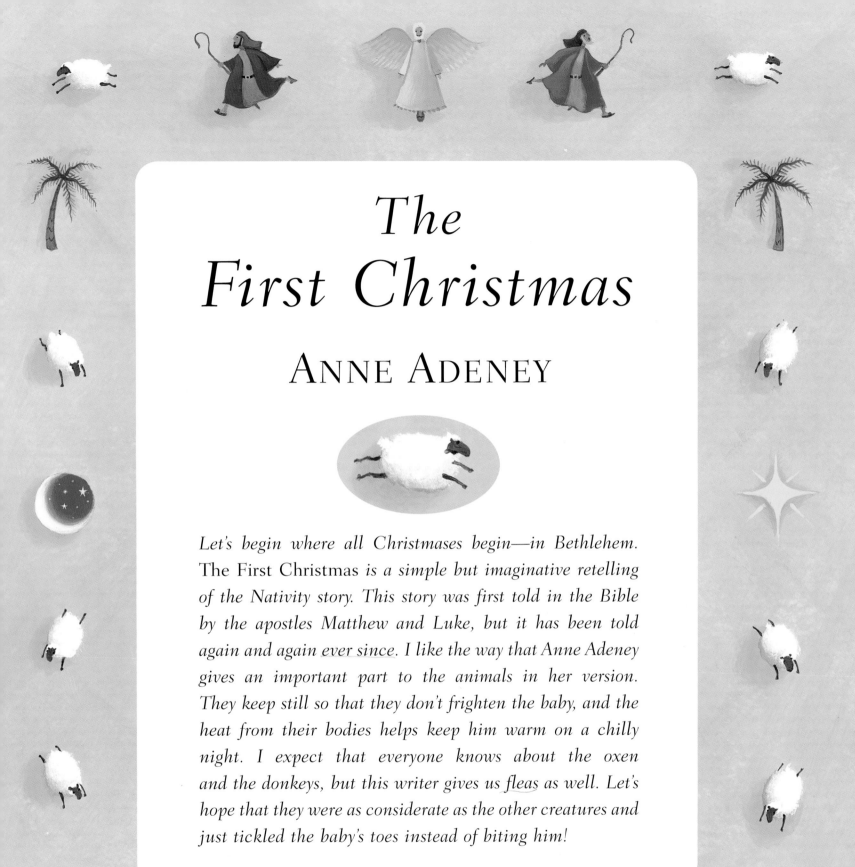

Let's begin where all Christmases begin—in Bethlehem. The First Christmas *is a simple but imaginative retelling of the Nativity story. This story was first told in the Bible by the apostles Matthew and Luke, but it has been told again and again ever since. I like the way that Anne Adeney gives an important part to the animals in her version. They keep still so that they don't frighten the baby, and the heat from their bodies helps keep him warm on a chilly night. I expect that everyone knows about the oxen and the donkeys, but this writer gives us fleas as well. Let's hope that they were as considerate as the other creatures and just tickled the baby's toes instead of biting him!*

It came to pass that the emperor, Caesar Augustus, ordered a census to be taken throughout the Roman Empire.

"Now at last I can ensure that I get all the taxes that are due to me," he said, rubbing his hands together greedily. "Send town and village in the empire. Every man must take his family and go to the town of his forefathers to have his name recorded."

Joseph, a carpenter from Nazareth, belonged to a royal bloodline. He was descended from the great King David, whose home had been the town of Bethlehem, in Judea. So Joseph made preparations to go to Bethlehem in order to register. His new wife, Mary, had to go with him, even though it was nearly time for her baby to be born. Nine months before, an angel had appeared to Mary and told her that she would have a baby by the Holy Spirit. That baby would be the Son of God.

It was 90 miles from Nazareth to Bethlehem—a long journey. It was winter, so the days were wet and chilly, and the nights were bitterly cold. As her donkey trudged down the rocky path, Mary hunched her shoulders against the biting wind and drew her blue headdress closer to her face. There was danger too, from bandits during the day, and wolves or other wild animals at night. But there were many families traveling south through the Jordan Valley to be registered. Mary and Joseph always kept close to the other travelers and eventually reached Bethlehem safely.

When they arrived, they found that the town was overflowing with people.

The crowds jostled and pushed, and Joseph was concerned for Mary. Even riding the donkey couldn't protect her from the crush in the streets. There were many other people riding donkeys, as well as much larger animals. The enormous camels of the rich merchants loped through the streets, and oxen pulled wooden carts loaded with firewood or goods to sell. There were even a few people on horseback, jostling anyone in their path as they passed.

"We'll find somewhere to stay right away," said Joseph.

He pushed his way through the crowded streets, holding the donkey's bridle. The townspeople were going about their business. Many worked just outside their homes. Some were making pottery, while others wove baskets and sandals. Mary and Joseph passed through the marketplace, which was buzzing with people buying and selling their wares, gossiping, and arguing. The couple also saw several Roman centurions on horseback. They kept order in the throng of people who had already lined up to give their details to the census taker.

Dotted along the roadside were families grouped around cooking fires, recovering from their long walk. But Joseph

was determined to find somewhere warm and sheltered for Mary. Although Joseph was only a poor carpenter, he had enough money saved to afford a night in a good lodging house. The holy baby deserved that at least. With his staff he knocked on the door of the first respectable place that he found. It was an impressive stone building with a wide wooden door.

"We need a room for the night," said Joseph when the door opened, the wonderful smell of rich food wafting out. The innkeeper was nearly as wide as the doorway. His handsome green robe stretched tightly across his great belly, which wobbled as he spoke.

"A room in Bethlehem, tonight?" he scoffed. "You must be joking! Don't you know that there's a census going on? I have no rooms left."

"We'll try another place," Joseph said to Mary. "We're sure to find somewhere soon."

They stopped at the next lodging house. It was smaller and set in a grove of gnarled olive trees. There was a narrow staircase leading up to the flat roof, where travelers could sleep in warmer weather. The tall, thin innkeeper shivered as a gust of wind tried to blow the door back into his face.

"Have you a room for us?" asked Joseph.

The innkeeper shook his head.

"Or even the corner of a room, out of this wind?" Joseph asked hopefully. "We have traveled such a long way, and we're cold and tired."

"I'm sorry, we have no room," said the innkeeper. "I doubt you'll find an empty space in all of Bethlehem."

Despite these words, Joseph kept on trying. He led Mary from place to place, searching for anywhere that had room for two weary travelers. But there was no room to be found. It was getting dark, and Mary knew the baby was about to arrive.

Desperate now, they came to the last building on the edge of the town. The small house was made of gray stone that was so old that it was crumbling around the edges. They could hear many voices murmuring inside.

"Is this an inn?" asked Mary.

"I'm not sure," said Joseph, "but I'll try here anyway. We must get you out of the cold before the baby comes."

He knocked on the narrow door.

"We have no room," said a voice, before Joseph could even open his mouth to ask. The short, bald man could barely open the door, there were so many people inside. "We even sent all the children to stay with their grandmother to make a little more space. But now we're full."

The strong smell of many people packed closely into a small space floated out on the chilly evening air. But Joseph and Mary did not mind that.

"Are you sure?" asked Joseph. "Forget about me, just find a place for Mary here. She really needs shelter."

"It's so crowded in here that even the fleas have left and gone down to the stable," the innkeeper said with a chuckle.

Joseph's eyes lit up. "Did you say you had a stable?"

The innkeeper took pity on them and led them to his stable. It was full of donkeys whose owners were lodged at the inn. There was even

an enormous ox. Joseph put down fresh straw for Mary and made her a bed in the corner.

Soon after Mary gave birth to her son and wrapped him in the swaddling clothes that she had brought with her. The animals stayed calm and still, even when Joseph put clean hay in the manger so it could be used as a bed for the baby. The animals' large, gentle eyes watched Mary and the baby intently. Their dusty bodies, all shades of brown and gray, gave off a heat that warmed and comforted the little family.

"We'll call him Jesus," said Mary contentedly, as she laid the baby in the manger. "Just as the angel told me to."

Outside Bethlehem some shepherds had gathered their sheep together for the night. Now that darkness had fallen like a blanket over the hills, most of them had settled down to sleep. They wrapped their sheepskin robes tightly around themselves to keep out the freezing cold. A few stayed awake, as usual, to guard the flock from wolves and mountain lions.

Suddenly, an angel of the Lord appeared from heaven, and the radiance of God's glory shone down on them, more brightly than the desert sun. All the shepherds woke up, terrified. But the angel reassured them.

"Do not be afraid!" he said. "I bring tidings of great joy for everyone! The Savior, your Messiah, has been born in Bethlehem! This is how you will recognize the Lord—you will find a baby wrapped in swaddling clothes and lying in a manger."

Then many thousands of angels appeared, and they filled the sky with songs of praise to God.

"Glory to God in the highest, and peace on earth to all who please God!"

When the angels had returned to heaven, the shepherds could not wait to find this holy baby.

"Let's go to Bethlehem!" said their leader. "The Lord has sent us news about this wonderful event, but let's go and see it for ourselves!"

They ran all the way to the town and soon found Mary and Joseph in the stable. And there was the baby in the manger, just as the angel had told them.

The tiny baby slept peacefully, with Mary and Joseph and the animals watching over him. Looking down at her baby son, Mary radiated a joy that outshone the moon and the stars above them.

Then the shepherds excitedly told them what the angels had said, proud that they had been the first ones to see the Messiah, the Savior of their people. Mary quietly treasured their words in her heart.

The innkeeper came down to see what all the commotion was about. Hearing the story, he ran to fetch the rest of the people in his house. All who heard about it were astonished. The shepherds glorified and praised God as they repeated the story to everyone who would listen. But at last the shepherds went back to find all their sheep still safe on the hillside, and Mary and Joseph settled down to sleep beside their precious baby.

This was the first Christmas.

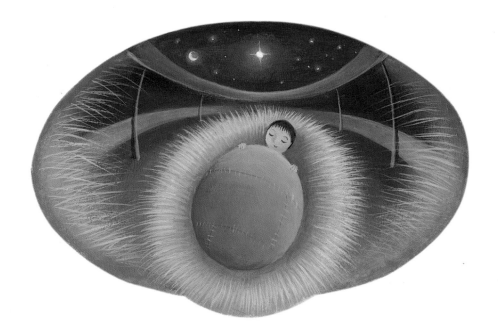

Old Pierre's Christmas Visitors

FIONA WATERS

This traditional French folktale is a reminder that Christmas is a time to think about those who are poorer and less fortunate than ourselves. The story has attracted many writers, including the greatest Russian writer of all, Leo Tolstoy, who wrote a version called Papa Panov. In Fiona Waters' retelling Old Pierre has a dream in which Jesus promises to meet him on Christmas day. At first there's no sign of Jesus, only of people who have fallen on hard times. As the old man tries to provide them with some comfort and relief, we begin to wonder whether he is ever going to meet his longed-for Savior. But there's a pleasant surprise in store for this warm-hearted man.

Old Pierre stood up slowly. His tired knees creaked, and his hand trembled as he leaned on his workbench to steady himself. Darkness had fallen outside, and the old shoemaker decided to finish work for the day. He walked stiffly to the door and stepped outside to put up the shutters.

It was Christmas Eve, and the street bustled with excited children and scurrying mothers frantically buying provisions for the festivities. Shafts of light from the shops spilled onto the snow-covered sidewalk, and faint smells of cooking swirled through the air.

Old Pierre shivered but not with the cold. He was thinking of Christmases past, when his beloved wife was alive and their children would dance happily around the kitchen. He sighed as he looked off into the distance. Now he was all on his own. Old Pierre banged the shutters closed and stumped back inside.

He lit a candle and helped himself to a bowl of soup from the big pot on the stove and then settled down in his deep armchair, with the family Bible on his lap. With his glasses perched on the end of his nose, he read the familiar words of the Christmas story—how Mary, worn out from traveling and close to the time her baby was to be born, settled in the stable with relief. Old Pierre sighed again. "If they had come here, I could have given them my bed and the big quilt to keep warm."

He read on to the arrival of the Wise Men and then frowned. "I would have no precious gift for the Christ Child," he said sadly. Suddenly he smiled. "Ah, but I do! I have just the right present!"

He put down his Bible and went to look under his workbench. He pushed several rolls of leather and old tools aside and pulled out a small box. Returning to his chair, he blew the dust off the lid and opened it. There lay the tiniest pair of shoes imaginable, the smallest and best that he had ever made. They would do.

As he gazed at the tiny shoes with satisfaction, his eyes grew heavy. Before he realized it, Old Pierre was fast asleep, his glasses still on the end of his nose. The candle burned all the way down. As he slept, Old Pierre had a wonderful dream. Someone was by his side, someone with a kind, gentle face and a warm, strong voice. It was Jesus.

"Old Pierre, look for me tomorrow. I will visit you, and you can provide for me as you wish. Be sure you recognize me." Then he was gone.

Old Pierre slept on peacefully, a smile on his tired old face, until the room became light and the bells began to peal joyfully. It was Christmas day!

Old Pierre shook himself awake. He was stiff from sitting for so long in his chair, and it took him a moment to get up. He opened the door, and the sound of the bells rang through the shop.

His heart filled with joy as he remembered his dream. Jesus was coming to visit! Old Pierre took down the shutters and looked around. More snow had fallen during the night, and it sparkled in the pale early morning sun. The street was completely empty.

"I wonder how Jesus will look," said Old Pierre to himself. "Will he come back as a baby or as a grown man? I must keep a sharp lookout." He went inside to put a fresh pot of coffee on the stove. But he couldn't settle down. What if he missed Jesus? He looked up and down the street, but there was no one to be seen. Well, not quite no one. Albert the road sweeper was there, hunched over his broom as usual. He looked chilled to the bone. Impulsively, Old Pierre called: "Albert, hey! Come inside and have some hot coffee to celebrate Christmas day!"

Albert shambled across the road, rubbing his hands together. His battered old boots scuffed the snow.

"Thank you, Pierre," he said with a grin. "It is very cold out there today." He sat by the fire and clasped his mug gratefully. Old Pierre smiled at the scruffy road sweeper but kept one eye on the road all the time. It would never do to keep his important guest waiting.

Albert looked at Old Pierre curiously. "Are you expecting someone?"

So Old Pierre told Albert about his dream.

Albert smiled. "Well, you have given me an unexpected treat. For your sake, Pierre, I hope your dream comes true." He gathered himself up and went back outside to continue sweeping up the snow. Old Pierre sat for a moment by the fire, thinking about Albert's words. Then he leaped to his feet again, peering out into the street. But there was no one to be seen. Well, not quite no one.

As he watched, someone walked very slowly toward his door. Old Pierre rushed out. It was a young woman clasping a bundle to her chest. She came closer, and Old Pierre saw that she was very pale and tired. The bundle was a tiny baby wrapped in a thin blanket. Without hesitating, Old Pierre stepped forward.

"My dear, you look frozen. Please come in and join me."

He led them into the house and pulled the deep armchair even closer to the fire. He warmed some milk, and while the young woman rested, he fed the tiny baby himself. Her little feet felt icy cold in his hands.

"She needs shoes!" he exclaimed in distress.

"I have no money for shoes. My husband is dead, and I am looking for work just so that we can buy enough food to survive," the young woman said quietly.

Old Pierre thought of the tiny shoes, his gift for Jesus. What should he do? If he gave the shoes to the baby, what would he give Jesus? But the little feet in his hands were very cold.

"Why don't you try these on her?" he said and handed the tiny shoes to the woman. With trembling fingers, she fastened the shoes onto her daughter's feet. They were a perfect fit.

With a huge smile, Old Pierre said, "Take them, my dear. They could have been made for her." Then he went to the stove and put the big pot on the heat so they could share a bowl of soup and some bread.

When she left some time later, the young woman placed a hand on Old Pierre's sleeve. "You will never know how much your kindness has meant to me and my baby. I hope all your Christmas wishes come true!" She waved as she walked off down the street.

Old Pierre still looked out of his window. The street was busy now. He saw some of his customers and many friends, as well as a little group of beggars, but there was no sign of the one special visitor he was waiting for. He looked again at the beggars. What was he thinking about? It was Christmas, after all. He made his way to the door again and invited the poor souls in for some soup and bread. All the while he kept an eye on the road in case he should miss Jesus.

Time passed, and dusk fell. The last of the beggars had gone, the last of the soup had been supped, and only a crust remained of the bread. Old Pierre was tired, and his heart was heavy. He looked one last time down the empty street. Then he put the shutters up again and came back to sit in the deep armchair. He looked sadly into the heart of the fire. Jesus had not come. It had just been a dream after all. His eyes misted with tears.

A soft, strange light filled the room. A voice said, "Did you really not see me, Old Pierre?"

It was the warm, strong voice from his dream. It was the voice of Jesus!

"I was hungry, and you gave me food. I was thirsty, and you gave me something to drink. I was cold and lonely, and you invited me into your house. I was barefoot, and you gave me shoes. Did you really not see me, Old Pierre?" the voice asked again.

Old Pierre knew this time that this was no dream. Jesus was here in the room with him. To his astonishment, Old Pierre saw a procession pass by his chair. First came Albert the road sweeper, then the young woman with her tiny baby, and then the troop of beggars.

"I was here today in everyone you welcomed into your house," said Jesus. "By helping them, you have indeed helped me."

Then there was silence, and the room was still. Old Pierre thought his heart would burst with joy.

"He did come after all!" he whispered.

The Elves and the Shoemaker

THE BROTHERS GRIMM

This story is one of a large number of German folktales collected by the Brothers Grimm in the early 1800s. As in Old Pierre's Christmas Visitors, the hero of this famous folktale is a shoemaker. Only this time it's the shoemaker himself who has fallen on hard times. Luckily, some elves turn up and help save the shoemaker's business, but when he and his wife try to repay the secretive little creatures, the elves abandon them. Thanks to the couple's continued hard work, however, their business thrives. I like the idea that it's their human determination and decency that has saved their business, not just magical elf stitching, don't you?

Once upon a time there was a shoemaker who worked hard and made very good shoes. All day he toiled in his shop, but times were hard, and he grew poorer and poorer. Finally the evening came when he cut out a pair of shoes from his last bit of leather. He put the pieces on his bench to sew in the morning when the light was better and laid everything out ready, including the needles and thread.

"I may never make another pair of shoes," he sighed as he put the shutters over the shop window. "When I sell these, I must use all the money to buy food for my family, and there will be nothing left over for more leather. Oh dear, what shall I do?"

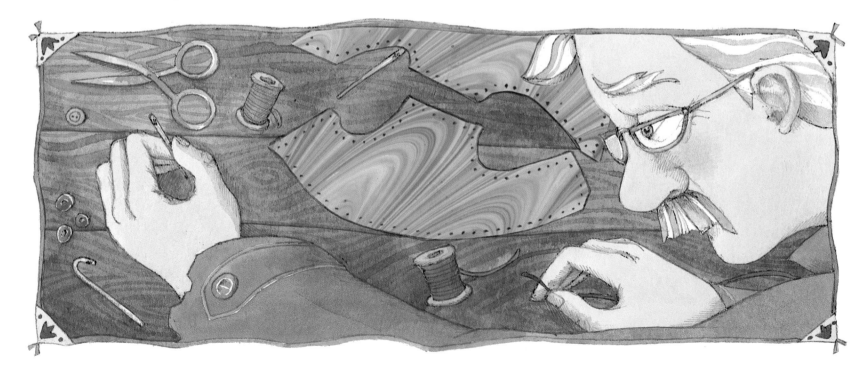

The next morning he awoke with a heavy heart and went sadly to his bench. To his amazement, instead of the pile of leather pieces, he found the most beautiful pair of shoes, exquisitely sewn with the tiniest, neatest stitches he had ever seen. The shoemaker was quite bewildered, but he took down his shutters and put the shoes in the shop window.

He was still puzzling over who could have made them when the door opened and in came a rich old gentleman. He wanted to buy the shoes and offered the shoemaker four times as much as he had ever been paid for a pair of shoes in his life. The shoemaker was overjoyed. He rushed straight out and bought more leather and enough food to feed his family for several days.

That evening he sat at his bench and cut out two pairs of shoes from the new leather. He left the pieces laid out as before, ready to sew the next day. In the morning he was even more amazed to find two beautiful pairs of shoes sitting on the bench.

"Whoever can it be," he wondered, "who works so fast and sews such tiny stitches?"

Again he put the shoes in the shop window, and rich people who had never visited his shop before came in and paid a lot of money for them. The shoemaker went off again and bought more leather and cut out more

shoes. Every night for weeks the same thing happened. Two pairs, sometimes four pairs, were made in a night, and the shoemaker was soon known all over the town for his excellent shoes.

But he still had no idea who was making the shoes, and he grew more curious day by day. One evening he could bear it no longer, and he and his wife stayed awake and peeped from behind the door to see who their helpful night visitors were. As the clock struck midnight, they heard a scuffling and a scurrying from the window and saw two little men squeezing through the shutters. They hurried over to the bench, took a set of tiny tools from their workbag, and began stitching and hammering. The shoemaker and his wife rubbed their eyes to make sure they weren't dreaming, for the little men were no bigger than the shoemaker's needles! The elves—for that is what they were—worked hard until just before dawn, when three beautiful pairs of shoes stood ready on the bench. Then they packed their tools away, cleaned up the mess, and vanished the way they had come.

When the shoemaker and his wife had recovered from their amazement, they wondered how they could show their gratitude to the elves. As it was just before Christmas, the shoemaker's wife suggested that they should make some tiny clothes as presents for the raggedy little fellows. So all the next day

she busied herself making two little green jackets and two pairs of trousers, while the shoemaker stitched two tiny pairs of shoes.

On Christmas Eve they laid the presents out on the shoemaker's bench together with two tiny glasses of wine and a plate of little cakes and biscuits. That night they kept watch again. The elves scrambled into the shop and climbed onto the bench as they had done before. When they saw the little green jackets and trousers and the tiny shoes, they shouted and jumped for joy. They put the clothes on; they drank the wine and ate the food; then they disappeared in a flash.

After Christmas the shoemaker still cut out shoes and left the pieces on his bench, but the elves never came back. They knew the shoemaker and his wife had seen them because the clothes were exactly the right size—and elves do not like to be seen by humans.

The shoemaker did not really mind, for his shop was now so famous that he had plenty of customers. His stitches were not as neat as the elves' stitches, but no one seemed to notice. He and his family were never poor again, and every year after that on Christmas Eve they would gather around the fire and drink a toast to the little elves who had helped them when times were hard.

A Very Big Cat

NORA CLARKE

Christmas is about visiting old friends and family—and sometimes making new friends, as this delightfully unlikely Norse folktale shows. In the story of The Elves and the Shoemaker *the little magic visitors provide a very welcome service. But in this tale fairy folk threaten to ruin a family's Christmas festivities. I think I know what most people would do if someone turned up on their doorstep on Christmas Eve in a snowstorm with a great big bear and asked for shelter! Wait a moment, though. Just in case it happens to you, ask yourself this question: Would you rather share your Christmas with a polar bear or with a crowd of trolls throwing your turkey around and blowing bubbles in your milk?*

Many years ago a hunter from the Northlands trapped a great white bear. It was such a fine bear that he decided to present it to the king of his country. So the man and the bear set out, even though it was winter and the snow was falling thick and fast. They trudged and trudged, but the king's palace was far away, and it began to get dark. The hunter was cold and weary. Suddenly, through the trees, he glimpsed a little cottage with lights a-shining.

"I'll ask for shelter for the night," he told the big white bear as he knocked on the door. It was opened by a tall, thin man with a very worried face.

"Please, may we come in? We are both very tired from trudging through the snow," said the hunter.

"Oh no, no," replied the man, whose name was Halvor.

"We are going to see the king, this fine bear and I. We only want to warm ourselves at your fire for the night."

"Impossible! You can't stay here." Halvor waved his arms around. "I'm sorry. I can't help you." The bear gave a sad little grunt, while the hunter shivered and stared at Halvor in surprise. He tried again.

"We don't need much room, and we won't disturb you. Please don't turn us away into the snow." But Halvor shook his head.

"I'm not an unkind man," he said. "I'd like to help you, but it's Christmas Eve,

a time of great trouble for me."
He opened the door wider.

"Look at my wife and my three children hurrying to get things ready for Christmas. See how sad and worried they look," Halvor went on. "They never enjoy Christmas because year after year the trolls come. Many, many trolls. They chase us out, throw our food around, and then break all the dishes. They tear down the decorations, they scream, they shout. Oh no, Christmas is not a happy time for us."

"Trolls!" exclaimed the hunter. "Trolls don't frighten us. Please let us into your warm house. Trolls won't bother us, will they, Bear?"

At last Halvor let them both in, and they slept in a warm corner near the stove. Halvor's wife had prepared a delicious dinner, and on Christmas day she put everything on the table, which the children decorated with holly and candles.

All of a sudden, quicker than a flash, the trolls
appeared. They came down the chimney, in through
the windows, under the door, and even up through
the floorboards. Some were tall, and some were
small. Some had long noses and no tails; some
had long tails and long ears. All of them were
very, very ugly. Halvor and his family grabbed
their warmest clothes and ran and locked
themselves in the woodshed.

Then those trolls attacked. They bellowed. They
screamed. They threw the turkey and vegetables
around and smashed the dishes. They squashed jelly
into the floor and blew bubbles in the milk. They
jumped on the table and paddled in the custard.
Some smaller trolls emptied jars of jam and rubbed
it all over the windows. The noise was terrible, but
the man and his bear watched quietly by the stove.

At last, when there was nothing left to damage, the naughtiest troll of all saw the big bear lying peacefully in the corner. He grabbed a sausage, pushed it on a fork, and waved it under the bear's nose.

"Pussycat, pussycat, have a sausage," he shouted in a silly voice. The bear sniffed. It was a good smell. Suddenly the troll pulled the sausage away, out of the bear's reach.

"Pussycat, pussycat, here you are." Again the troll waved the sausage in front of the bear, and again he snatched it away. Slowly the bear lumbered to his feet. He opened his mouth wider and wider. He let out a great roar and then another even louder one. He chased those trolls up the chimney, out of the windows, and under the floorboards, from the smallest to the largest, until there was not one left.

"You are a fine bear," the hunter said proudly. "Here, have a sausage or two." So the bear ate sausages. Then he licked some jam from the windows, because bears love sweet things.

"You can come out of the woodshed now," the hunter shouted. "My bear has chased away all of the trolls!"

Halvor, his wife, and their three children crept back to the cottage. They could hardly believe that the trolls had gone, but when they saw it was true, they began cleaning up the mess in a hurry. There was still enough food left for a good supper before they all went to bed, and the next day the hunter and the bear went on their way to the king.

Halvor never saw them again.

A year later, on Christmas Eve, Halvor was chopping wood in the forest when he heard someone calling his name.

"Halvor! Halvor!"

"Yes, I'm Halvor. What do you want?" he replied.

"Is that big white cat still living with you?" It was a troll's voice.

"She certainly is," shouted Halvor. "And she has seven kittens now, each one bigger and fiercer than the last. Do you want to visit her?"

"No! We'll never come to your house again," the trolls screamed. And they never did. Forever afterward Halvor, his wife, and their three children enjoyed their Christmas day in peace and contentment.

Becky's Christmas Dream

LOUISA MAY ALCOTT

Louisa May Alcott's books—the best known of which is Little Women—reflect her strong sense that the way to be happy is through love, hard work, and doing one's duty. Becky's Christmas Dream, first published in 1870, is her own version of the Cinderella story. A poor little orphan girl is left alone while the family she works for is out. At first she feels lonely and afraid, but because it's Christmas Eve, she discovers that for one magical hour she can talk with things that normally don't have voices. By the time her mistress gets home with her children, Becky has had some wonderful advice that helps her overcome all her problems.

All alone, by the kitchen fire, sat little Becky, for everyone else had gone away to keep Christmas, and left her to take care of the house. Nobody had thought to give her any presents, or take her to any merry-making, or remembered that Christmas should be made a happy time to every child, whether poor or rich. She was only twelve years old – this little girl from the poorhouse, who was bound to work for the farmer's wife till she was eighteen. She had no father or mother, no friends or home but this, and as she sat alone by the fire her little heart ached for someone to love and cherish her.

Becky was a shy, quiet child, with a thin face and wistful eyes that always seemed to be trying to find something which she wanted very much. She worked away, day after day, so patiently and silently that no one ever guessed what curious thoughts filled the little cropped head, or what a tender child's heart was hidden under the blue checked pinafore.

Tonight she was wishing that there were fairies in the world, who would whisk down the chimney and give her quantities of pretty things, as they did in the delightful fairy tales.

"I'm sure I am as poor and lonely as Cinderella, and need a kind godmother to help me as much as ever she did," said Becky to herself as she sat on her little stool staring at the fire, which didn't burn very well, for she felt too much out of sorts to care whether things looked cheerful or not.

There is an old belief that all dumb things can speak for one hour on Christmas Eve. Now, Becky knew nothing of the story, and no one can say whether what happened was true, or whether she fell asleep and dreamed it all. But certain it is, when Becky compared herself to Cinderella, she was amazed to hear a small voice reply: "Well, my dear, if you want advice I shall be very glad to give you some, for I've had much experience in this trying world."

Becky stared about her, but all she saw was the old grey cat, blinking at the fire.

"Did you speak, Tabby?" said the child, at last.

"Of course I did. If you wish a godmother, here I am."

Becky laughed at the idea; but Puss, with her silver-grey suit, white handkerchief crossed on her bosom, kind, motherly old face, and cosy purr, did make a very good, Quakerish little godmother after all.

"Well, ma'am, I'm ready to listen," said Becky, respectfully.

"First, my child, what do you want most?" asked the godmother, quite in the fairy-book style.

"To be loved by everybody," answered Becky.

"Good!" said the cat. "I'm pleased with that answer; it's sensible; and I'll tell you how to get your wish. Learn to make people love you by loving them."

"I don't know how," sighed Becky.

"No more did I, in the beginning," returned Puss. "When I first came here, a shy young kitten, I thought only of keeping out of everybody's way, for I was afraid of everyone. I hid under the barn, and only came out when no one was near. I wasn't happy, for I wanted to be petted, but didn't know how to begin.

"One day I heard Aunt Sally say to the master: 'James, that wild kitten ain't no use at all; you'd better drown her, and get a nice tame one to amuse the children and clear the house of mice.'

"'The poor thing has been abused, I guess; so we'll give her another trial, and maybe she'll come to trust us after a while,' said the good master.

"I thought over these things as I lay under the barn and resolved to do my best, for I didn't wish to be drowned. It was hard at first; but I began by coming out when little Jane called me, and letting her play with me. Then I ventured into the house, and finding a welcome at my first visit, I went again and took a mouse with me, to show that I wasn't idle.

"No one hurt or frightened me, and soon I was the household pet. For several years I have led a happy life here."

Becky listened intently, and when Puss ended, she said, timidly, "Do you think if I try not to be afraid, but to show that I want to be affectionate, the people will let me and will like it?"

"Very sure. I heard the mistress say you were a good, handy little thing. Do as I did, my dear, and you will find that there is plenty of love in the world."

"I will; thank you, dear old Puss, for your advice."

Puss came to rub her soft cheek against Becky's hand, and then settled herself in a cosy hunch in Becky's lap. Presently another voice spoke – a queer, monotonous voice, high above her.

"Tick, tick; wish again, little Becky, and I'll tell you how to find your wish."

It was the old moon-faced clock behind the door, which had struck twelve just before Tabby first spoke.

"Dear me," said Becky, "how queerly things do act tonight!" She thought a moment, then said, soberly, "I wish I liked my work better; but washing dishes, picking chips and hemming towels is such tiresome work, I don't see how I can go on doing it for six more years."

"Just what I used to feel," said the clock. "I couldn't bear to think that I had got to stand here and do nothing but tick year after year. I flatly said I wouldn't, and I stopped half a dozen times a day. Bless me, what a fuss I made, until I was

put in this corner to stand idle for several months. At first I rejoiced; then I got tired of doing nothing, and began to reflect that as I was born a clock, it would be wiser to do my duty and get some satisfaction out of it if I could."

"And so you went to going again – please teach me to be faithful, and to love my duty," cried Becky.

"I will," and the old clock grandly struck the half-hour, with a smile on its round face as it ticked steadily on and on.

Here the fire blazed up, and the tea-kettle, hanging on the crane, began to sing.

"How cheerful that is!" said Becky, as the whole kitchen brightened with the ruddy glow. "If I could have a third wish, I'd wish to be as cheerful as the fire."

"Have your wish if you choose; but you must work for it, as I do," cried the fire, as its flames embraced the old kettle till it gurgled with pleasure.

Becky thought she heard a queer voice humming these words:

"I'm an old black kettle,
With a very crooked nose,
But I can't help being gay
When the jolly fire glows."

"I shouldn't wonder a mite if that little no-good had been up to mischief tonight, rummaged all over the house, ate herself sick, or stole something and run away with it," croaked Aunt Sally, as the family went jingling home in the big sleigh about one o'clock from the Christmas party.

"Tut, tut, Aunty, I wouldn't think evil of the thing. If I'd had my way, she'd have gone with us and had a good time. She don't look as if she'd seen many. I've a notion it's what she needs," said the farmer kindly.

"The thought of her alone at home has worried me all the evening; but she didn't seem to mind, and I haven't had time to get a decent dress ready for her, so I let it go," added the farmer's wife, as she cuddled little Jane under the cloaks and shawls, with a regretful memory of Becky knocking at her heart.

"I've got some popcorn and a bouncing big apple for her," said Billy, the red-faced lad perched up by his father playing driver.

"And I'll give her one of my dolls. She said she never had one – wasn't that dreadful?" put in little Jane, popping out her head like a bird from its nest.

"Better see what she has been about fust," advised Aunt Sally. "But if she hasn't done no mischief, and has remembered to have the kettle bilin' so I can have a warm cup of tea after my ride, and if she's kep' the fire up, and het my slippers, I don't know but I'll give her the red mittens I knit."

They found poor Becky lying on the bare floor, her head pillowed on the stool, and old Tabby in her arms with a corner of the blue pinafore spread over her. The fire was burning splendidly, the kettle simmering, and in a row upon the hearth stood, not only Aunt Sally's old slippers, but those of master and mistress also, and over a chair hung two little nightgowns, warming for the children.

"Well, now, if that don't beat all for thoughtfulness and sense! Becky shall have them mittens, and I'll knit her a couple of pair of stockin's as sure as she's livin'," said Aunt Sally, completely won by this unusual proof of "forehandedness" in a servant.

So Aunt Sally laid the gay mittens close to the little rough hand that worked so busily all day. Billy set his big red apple and bag of popcorn just where she would see them when she woke. Jane laid the doll in Becky's arms, and Tabby smelt of it approvingly, to the children's delight. The farmer had no present ready, but he stroked the little cropped head with a fatherly touch that made Becky smile in her sleep, as he said within himself, "I'll do by this forlorn child as I'd wish anyone to do by my Janey if she was left alone."

But the mother gave the best gift of all, for she stooped down and kissed Becky as only mothers can kiss, for the good woman's heart reproached her for neglect of the child who had no mother.

That unusual touch waked Becky at once, and looking about her with astonished eyes, she saw such a wonderful change in all the faces that her own lost its pathetic sadness as she clapped her hands and cried with a child's happy laugh –

"My dream's come true! O, my dream's come true!"

The Nutcracker

ANTONIA BARBER

For many families nowadays a visit to the ballet is a special Christmas treat. Everyone loves The Nutcracker, with its spectacular moonlit scenes of battling mice, toy soldiers, and a fabulous, dancing Sugar Plum Fairy. Here's a chance to read a retelling of the German tale by E. T. A. Hoffman that inspired the dreamlike ballet. What's interesting for me is its reminder that Christmas can be frightening for children if it becomes a grand social affair for adults. We begin with our heroine, Clara, hiding behind a curtain to escape the Grand Ball that her parents have organized. Later that night she dreams herself to be in the place where every child wants to be at this time of the year— the Land of Sweets.

Clara knelt on the window seat, half hidden by the heavy curtains, and pressed her nose against the cold glass of the window. Outside the night was still and full of mystery, with great feathery flakes of snow falling silently out of a dark sky. Behind her, the room was bright and warm and full of cheerful sounds.

Each year, on the night before Christmas, Clara's parents gave a splendid party and invited all their friends, old and young, to join in the celebrations. They were friendly people who liked nothing better than to fill their house with happy guests. But Clara, who was shy and awkward with strangers, found it all a little frightening. So it was that she was hiding behind the curtain, wishing that she could fly out of the window into the quiet darkness and float magically over the rooftops with their soft white blanket of snow.

Reflected in the glass she could see the moving shapes of people dancing and, beyond them, the glow of the big Christmas tree in the far corner of the room.

"Clara! Why are you hiding there?" She sighed as her brother, Franz, came bouncing onto the window seat. He took hold of her hand and pulled her down into the noisy room.

"Oh, Franz!" she protested. "Can't you leave me in peace?"

"No, I can't," he said, "because Mother has sent me to find you.

She has some friends who have just arrived, and they want to see you."

Clara reluctantly went with him to find her mother; then she stood patiently while people patted her on the head and said how much she had grown. They all looked very much alike to her, the men in their fine clothes, the women in their silken dresses; until the last visitor arrived. He was quite different: a strange man, old and bent, he was dressed all in black and had a dark patch over one eye.

Clara's parents greeted him with affection, and he did not pat her on the head or say that she had grown. Instead he fixed his one bright eye upon her and said, very softly, "Ah . . . this one is special."

Behind the old man came servants carrying tall boxes. The guests crowded around to see what could be inside, and there were cries of wonder when they were opened. Out came a tall soldier and a pretty girl, followed by a Harlequin and a Columbine. They were life-size dolls, and

when the old man wound them up with a huge key, they danced together to the delight of the guests. The children tried to join in and, when the dancing was over, clamored for the dolls to be wound up again. But instead the lights were dimmed so that the Christmas tree could be seen shining in all its glory, and from beneath it Clara's parents took presents for all their friends.

As the children opened their beautifully wrapped packages, Clara felt a hand upon her shoulder and turned to see the strange old man holding out to her an oddly shaped toy.

"This is a special gift," he said, "given only to one who will know its true value." It was an ugly wooden doll with long thin legs, little short arms, and a head far too big for its body. It had a funny face and a mouth full of big teeth. It was certainly not a pretty toy, but there was something so comical about it that Clara loved it at first sight. She turned to the old man with a smile that lit up her face.

"Oh, thank you," she said. "I think he's lovely!"

"He is useful, too," said the old man, and he reached for a nut from a piled dish nearby. Taking the doll from Clara, he showed her how to fit the nut between the big teeth and crack it by squeezing the legs together. Clara was enchanted and so were the other children who crowded around, begging her to crack nuts for them. But Franz grew jealous; he hated to see his sister be the center of attention.

Suddenly, he snatched the Nutcracker from her hands and, throwing the wooden doll upon the floor, jumped on it. Clara was in tears until her father came to the rescue. He threatened to send Franz to bed if he did not behave himself and restored the battered toy to Clara. Poor Nutcracker! His paint was scratched, and his wood was dented. His comical face was more lopsided and ugly than ever, but Clara only loved him more.

She bandaged him with the white ribbon from her hair and, rocking him in her arms, she crept back to her hiding place behind the window curtain. The party lasted late into the night, with tired children sleeping where they fell, until their parents gathered them up to take them home.

When all the guests were gone, Franz and Clara were carried up to their nursery to be tucked into their beds. As her father lifted the sleeping Clara from her window seat, the battered Nutcracker fell from her hands and was left behind unnoticed on the floor. The lights went out, the fire died down. Time passed, and the whole house grew dark and still.

Clara awoke suddenly in the middle of the night: it took her a few moments to realize that she was in her bed. She sat up and felt around her for the Nutcracker, but he was nowhere to be found. She thought of him, lying alone in the great drawing room downstairs, and she could not bear it.

Climbing out of her warm bed, she put on her slippers and tiptoed across the nursery. The moon had come out, and as she went down the wide, cold staircase, she could see the world beyond the landing window shining with a snowy brightness. The white light lit up the darkened house and showed her the way. Softly, she turned the handle of the drawing room door. As she swung it open, the draft made the dying fire flare up, filling the room with dancing shadows. Crossing the wide, empty room, she heard a sudden scuttling sound, and a mouse ran across the floor. Clara was frightened of mice, especially in the middle of the night, so she gathered up her nightgown and raced to the safety of the window seat. Leaning down, she picked up the Nutcracker and hugged him tight.

It was cozy on the window seat; she felt safe there, and she did not like the long walk back to her room, not with mice running around the house. She pulled up the warm velvet curtain to cover herself, put her head down on the soft cushion, and closed her eyes.

It seemed only a moment later that she heard a strange scratching noise. Opening her eyes, she found the familiar drawing room mysteriously changed. Everything seemed much larger, the spaces vast, the Christmas tree looming above her like a forest giant. *It is magic*, she thought a little breathlessly, *and in magic anything can happen.*

The scratching sound grew louder, and to Clara's horror, a horde of big, fierce mice came scurrying out of the shadows into the dancing firelight. They ran swiftly all over the room, nibbling at the gingerbread men on the Christmas tree, who had to scramble higher in an effort to escape them. Even worse, she saw a huge rat with a crown on his head, who seemed to be their king. Poor Clara, her heart beat fast, and her hands trembled with fear that he might notice her in her dark corner.

Then she heard the sound of a trumpet, and out from a big box marched a troop of toy soldiers, waving their wooden swords in the air. Their leader seemed strangely familiar, with a big head and long, thin legs. Clara realized with astonishment that it was her own dear Nutcracker, come to life.

She watched, holding her breath, as a fierce battle took place between the toy soldiers and the mice. Backward and forward they fought across the drawing room floor, until at last the soldiers drove the mice back to their holes. Only the King Rat and the Nutcracker remained, locked in a deadly duel, and it seemed to Clara that the rat was winning. He had a fierce, sharp little sword, while the Nutcracker had only a wooden one. Suddenly the King Rat raised his sword as if he would strike to kill. Clara cried out and, taking off her slipper, threw it with all her strength. It hit the King Rat in the small of his back, knocking him off balance, and at once the Nutcracker brought the wooden sword down upon his head. The big rat lay still upon the floor until the mice came out, squeaking sorrowfully, and carried him away into their mouse hole.

Clara turned back to the Nutcracker and saw
to her surprise that his strange, big head
and long, thin legs had changed. Smiling
at her and holding out her slipper was
a young and handsome prince.

He knelt at Clara's feet and, while
he placed the slipper on again, he
thanked her for saving his life
and for breaking the spell that
had bound him.

"Once I lived in the Land of
Sweets," he told her, "until the terrible
day when I fell under a spell and was
doomed to spend my days as the ugly
Nutcracker. Only when my life was saved
by one who loved me in spite of my strange
looks could the spell be broken."

I think I must be dreaming, thought Clara wonderingly. But if she was,
she certainly did not want the dream to end.

"Now you must tell me your dearest wish," said the Nutcracker
Prince, "and I shall grant it."

At first Clara could not think what to ask for, but then she remembered
how she had longed to fly over the moonlit, snow-covered world
beyond the window. She told the Nutcracker Prince of her dream, and
at once he took her by the hand. A moment later she found herself

flying through a cloud of whirling snowflakes into a strange and magical world.

"I will take you to my own kingdom," said the Prince, and they swooped and soared through clouds and over snowcapped forests until, in the distance, they could see the white pinnacles of a powdered sugar castle rising up out of the snow. As they flew in through the great doorway, she saw that it had columns made of candy canes and that it was decorated with all the sweets she loved best.

Then it seemed to her that all the sweets were really alive and joyfully welcomed the Nutcracker Prince on his return.

The Prince presented Clara to the beautiful Sugar Plum Fairy, who ruled as queen over the Land of Sweets. He told how she had saved his life and freed him from the magic spell. When they heard this, all the sweets began to dance for joy, and Clara found that she was dancing with them. Around and around they went, faster and faster, until Clara grew breathless, and her head was in a whirl. Then suddenly the sounds and music died, all was quiet and still, and Clara awoke to the first pale light of Christmas morning.

Her first fear was that her friend the Nutcracker would be gone forever. Anxiously she looked around, but there he was on the window seat, as ugly and as comical as before. She picked him up and hugged him. "Perhaps it was magic," she told him, "or perhaps it was just a dream. But whichever it was, I shall always know that you are really a handsome prince inside."

And, clutching him in her arms, she set off back to her bedroom before the others should wake and find her missing.

Christmas Every Day

WILLIAM DEAN HOWELLS

Older children will probably know the Midas story—about the king who wanted everything he touched to turn to gold. Well, this is a version of that story, told with great charm and humor for American readers in 1892. It features a heroine who, instead of wanting to be rich, wants it to be Christmas all the time. Did you ever want that to happen? I know I did, especially in mid-December, when I started suffering the torture of counting down the long, restless nights before Santa arrived. I hope you'll find it interesting, as I did, to see what it was that American children liked to eat and to receive as presents at Christmas more than one hundred years ago.

The little girl came into her papa's study, as she always did Saturday morning before breakfast, and asked for a story. He tried to beg off that morning, for he was very busy, but she would not let him.

So he began:

"Well, once there was a little pig – "

She stopped him at the word. She said she had heard little-pig stories till she was perfectly sick of them.

"Well, what kind of story shall I tell, then?"

"About Christmas. It's getting to be the season."

"Well!" Her papa roused himself. "Then I'll tell you about the little girl that wanted it Christmas every day in the year. How would you like that?"

"First-rate!" said the little girl; and she nestled into a comfortable shape in his lap, ready for listening.

"Very well, then, this little pig – oh, what are you pounding me for?"

"Because you said little pig instead of little girl."

"I should like to know what's the difference between a little pig and a little girl that wanted it Christmas every day!"

"Papa!" said the little girl warningly. At this, her papa began to tell the story.

Once there was a little girl who liked Christmas so much that she wanted it to be Christmas every day in the year, and as soon as Thanksgiving was over she began to send postcards to the old Christmas Fairy to ask if she mightn't have it. But the old Fairy never answered, and after a while the little girl found out that the Fairy wouldn't notice anything but real letters sealed outside with a monogram – or your initial, anyway. So, then she began to send letters, and just the day before Christmas, she got a letter from the Fairy, saying she might have it Christmas every day for a year, and then they would see about having it longer.

The little girl was excited already, preparing for the old-fashioned, once-a-year Christmas that was coming the next day. So she resolved to keep the Fairy's promise to herself and surprise everybody with it as it kept coming true, but then it slipped out of her mind altogether.

She had a splendid Christmas. She went to bed early, so as to let Santa Claus fill the stockings, and in the morning she was up the first of anybody and found hers all lumpy with packages of candy, and oranges and grapes, and rubber balls, and all kinds of small presents. Then she waited until the rest of the family was up, and she burst into the library to look at the large presents laid out on the library table – books, and boxes of stationery, and dolls, and little stoves, and dozens of handkerchiefs, and inkstands, and skates, and photograph frames, and boxes of watercolours, and dolls' houses – and the big Christmas tree, lighted and standing in the middle.

She had a splendid Christmas all day. She ate so much candy that she did not want any breakfast, and the whole forenoon the presents kept pouring in that had not been delivered the night before, and she went round giving the presents she had got for other people, and came home and ate turkey and cranberry for dinner, and plum pudding and nuts and raisins and oranges, and then went out and coasted, and came in with a stomach ache, crying, and her papa said he would see if his house was turned into that sort of fool's paradise another year, and they had a light supper, and pretty early everybody went to bed cross.

The little girl slept very heavily and very late, but she was wakened at last by the other children dancing around her bed with their stockings full of presents in their hands. "Christmas! Christmas! Christmas!" they all shouted.

"Nonsense! It was Christmas yesterday," said the little girl, rubbing her eyes sleepily.

Her brothers and sisters just laughed. "We don't know about that. It's Christmas today, anyway. You come into the library and see."

Then all at once it flashed on the little girl that the Fairy was keeping her promise, and her year of Christmases was beginning. She was dreadfully sleepy, but she sprang up and darted into the library. There it was again! Books, and boxes of stationery, and dolls, and so on.

There was the Christmas tree blazing away, and the family picking out their presents, and her father looking perfectly puzzled, and her mother ready to cry. "I'm sure I don't see how I'm to dispose of all these things," said her mother, and her father said it seemed to him they had had something just like it the day before, but he supposed he must have dreamed it.

This struck the little girl as the best kind of a joke, and so she ate so much candy she didn't want any breakfast, and went round carrying presents, and had turkey and cranberry for dinner, and then went out and coasted, and came in with a stomach ache, crying.

Now, the next day, it was the same thing over again, but everybody getting crosser, and at the end of a week's time so many people had lost their tempers that you could pick up lost tempers anywhere; they perfectly strewed the ground. Even when people tried to recover their tempers they usually got somebody else's, and it made the most dreadful mix.

The little girl began to get frightened, keeping the secret all to herself; she wanted to tell her mother, but she didn't dare to, and she was ashamed to ask the Fairy to take back her gift – it seemed ungrateful and ill-bred. So it went on and on, and it was Christmas on St Valentine's Day and Washington's Birthday, just the same as any day, and it didn't skip even the First of April, though everything was counterfeit that day, and that was some little relief.

After a while turkeys got to be awfully scarce, selling for about a thousand dollars apiece. They got to passing off almost anything as turkeys – even half-grown hummingbirds. And cranberries – well, they asked a diamond apiece for cranberries. All the woods and orchards were cut down for Christmas trees. After a while they had to make Christmas trees out of rags. But there were plenty of rags, because people got so poor, buying presents for one another, that they couldn't get any new clothes, and they just wore their

old ones to tatters. They got so poor that everybody had to go to the poorhouse, except the confectioners, and the storekeepers, and the booksellers, and they all got so rich and proud that they would hardly wait upon a person when he came to buy. It was perfectly shameful!

After it had gone on about three or four months, the little girl, whenever she came into the room in the morning and saw those great ugly, lumpy stockings dangling at the fireplace, and the disgusting presents around everywhere, used to sit down and burst out crying. In six months she was perfectly exhausted; she couldn't even cry any more.

And how it was on the Fourth of July! On the Fourth of July, the first boy in the United States woke up and found out that his firecrackers and toy pistol and two-dollar collection of fireworks were nothing but sugar and candy painted up to look like fireworks. Before ten o'clock every boy in the United States discovered that his July Fourth things had turned into Christmas things and was so mad. The Fourth of July orations all turned into Christmas carols, and when anybody tried to read the Declaration of Independence, instead of saying, "When in the course of human events it becomes necessary", he was sure to sing, "God rest you merry gentlemen". It was perfectly awful.

About the beginning of October the little girl took to sitting down on dolls wherever she found them – she hated the sight of them so – and by Thanksgiving she just slammed her presents across the room. By that time people didn't carry presents around nicely any more. They flung them over the fence or through the window, and instead of taking great pains to write: "For dear Papa" or "Mama" or "Brother" or "Sister", they used to write: "Take it, you horrid old thing!" and then go and bang it against the front door.

Nearly everybody had built barns to hold their presents, but pretty soon the barns overflowed, and then they used to let them lie out in the rain, or anywhere. Sometimes the police used to come and tell them to shovel their presents off the sidewalk or they would arrest them.

Before Thanksgiving came it leaked out who had caused all these Christmases. The little girl had suffered so much that she had talked about it in her sleep, and after that hardly anybody would play with her, because if it had not been for her greediness it wouldn't have happened. And now, when it came to be Thanksgiving, and she wanted them to go to church, and have turkey, and

show their gratitude, they said that all the turkeys had been eaten for her old Christmas dinners and if she would stop the Christmases, they would see about the gratitude. And the very next day the little girl began sending letters to the Christmas Fairy, and then telegrams, to stop it. But it didn't do any good, and then she got to calling at the Fairy's house, but the girl that came to the door always said, "Not at home", or "Engaged", or something like that, and so it went on till it came to the old once-a-year Christmas Eve. The little girl fell asleep, and when she woke up in the morning –

"She found it was all nothing but a dream," suggested the little girl.

"No indeed!" said her papa. "It was all every bit true!"

"What did she find out, then?"

"Why, that it wasn't Christmas at last, and wasn't ever going to be, anymore. Now it's time for breakfast."

The little girl held her papa fast around the neck.

"You shan't go if you're going to leave it so!"

"How do you want it left?"

"Christmas once a year."

"All right," said her papa, and he went on again.

Well, with no Christmas ever again, there was the greatest rejoicing all over the country. People met together everywhere and kissed and cried for joy. Carts went around and gathered up all the candy and raisins and nuts, and dumped them into the river, and it made the fish perfectly sick. And the whole United States, as far out as Alaska, was one blaze of bonfires, where the children were burning up their presents of all kinds. They had the greatest time!

The little girl went to thank the old Fairy because she had stopped its being Christmas, and she said she hoped the Fairy would keep her promise and see that Christmas never, never came again. Then the Fairy frowned, and said that now the little girl was behaving just as greedily as ever, and she'd better look out. This made the little girl think it all over carefully again, and she said she would be willing to have it Christmas about once in a thousand years, and then she said a hundred, and then she said ten, and at last she got down to one. Then the Fairy said that was the good old way that had pleased people ever since Christmas began, and she was agreed. Then the little girl said,

"What're your shoes made of?" And the Fairy said, "Leather." And the little girl said, "Bargain's done forever," and skipped off, and hippity-hopped the whole way home, she was so glad.

"How will that do?" asked the papa.

"First-rate!" said the little girl, but she hated to have the story stop, and was rather sober. However, her mama put her head in at the door and asked her papa: "Are you never coming to breakfast? What have you been telling that child?"

"Oh, just a tale with a moral."

The little girl caught him around the neck again.

"We know! Don't you tell what, papa! Don't you tell what!"

The Cratchits' Christmas Dinner

CHARLES DICKENS

Charles Dickens' classic novel, A Christmas Carol, *tells the story of Scrooge, a dreadful old miser. He is visited by the ghost of his deceased business partner and warned that if he doesn't change his ways, he'll die a miserable, lonely death. In this extract the Spirit of Christmas Present shows Scrooge the Christmas dinner being enjoyed by his employee, Bob Cratchit, and his family. This is the original English Christmas feast with all the trimmings—the goose, the gush of stuffing, the Christmas pudding (a steamed spongy dessert made of fruits and spices). And how the Cratchit family enjoys it, even though their poverty and Tiny Tim's bad health give them very little to celebrate.*

Then up rose Mrs Cratchit, Cratchit's wife, dressed out but poorly in a twice-turned gown, but brave in ribbons, which are cheap and make a goodly show for sixpence; and she laid the cloth, assisted by Belinda Cratchit, second of her daughters, also brave in ribbons; while Master Peter Cratchit plunged a fork into the saucepan of potatoes, and getting the corners of his monstrous shirt-collar (Bob's private property, conferred upon his son and heir in honour of the day) into his mouth, rejoiced to find himself so gallantly attired, and yearned to show his linen in the fashionable Parks. And now two smaller Cratchits, boy and girl, came tearing in, screaming that outside the baker's they had smelt the goose, and known it for their own; and basking in luxurious thoughts of sage and onion, these young Cratchits danced about the table, and exalted Master Peter Cratchit to the skies, while he (not proud, although his collars nearly choked him) blew the fire, until the slow potatoes, bubbling up, knocked loudly at the saucepan-lid to be let out and peeled.

"What has ever got your precious father, then?" said Mrs Cratchit. "And your brother, Tiny Tim? And Martha warn't as late last Christmas Day by half an hour!"

"Here's Martha, mother!" said a girl, appearing as she spoke.

"Here's Martha, mother!" cried the two young Cratchits. "Hurrah! There's such a goose, Martha!"

"Why, bless your heart alive, my dear, how late you are!" said Mrs Cratchit, kissing her a dozen times, and taking off her shawl and bonnet for her with officious zeal.

"We'd a deal of work to finish up last night," replied the girl, "and had to clear away this morning, mother!"

"Well! Never mind so long as you are come," said Mrs Cratchit. "Sit ye down before the fire, my dear, and have a warm, Lord bless ye!"

"No, no! There's father coming," cried the two young Cratchits, who were everywhere at once. "Hide, Martha, hide!"

So Martha hid herself, and in came little Bob, the father, with at least three feet of comforter, exclusive of the fringe, hanging down before him; and his threadbare clothes darned up and brushed to look seasonable, and Tiny Tim upon his shoulder. Alas for Tiny Tim, he bore a little crutch, and had his limbs supported by an iron frame!

"Why, where's our Martha?" cried Bob Cratchit, looking round.

"Not coming," said Mrs Cratchit.

"Not coming!" said Bob, with a sudden declension in his high spirits; for he had been Tim's blood-horse all the way from church, and had come home rampant. "Not coming upon Christmas Day!"

Martha didn't like to see him disappointed, if it were only in joke; so she came out prematurely from behind the closet door, and ran into his arms, while the two young Cratchits hustled Tiny Tim, and bore him off to the wash-house, that he might hear the pudding singing in the copper.

"And how did little Tim behave?" asked Mrs Cratchit, when she had rallied Bob on his credulity, and Bob had hugged his daughter to his heart's content.

"As good as gold," said Bob, "and better. Somehow, he gets thoughtful, sitting by himself so much, and thinks the strangest things you ever heard. He told me, coming home, that he hoped the people saw him in the church, because he was a cripple, and it might be pleasant to them to remember upon Christmas Day who made lame beggars walk and blind men see."

Bob's voice was tremulous when he told them this, and trembled more when he said that Tiny Tim was growing strong and hearty.

His active little crutch was heard upon the floor, and back came Tiny Tim before another word was spoken, escorted by his brother and sister to his stool beside the fire; and while Bob, turning up his cuffs – as if, poor fellow, they were capable of being made more shabby – compounded some hot mixture in a jug with gin and lemons, and stirred it round and round and put it on the hob to simmer, Master Peter and the two ubiquitous young Cratchits went to fetch the goose, with which they soon returned in high procession.

Such a bustle ensued that you might have thought a goose the rarest of all birds; a feathered phenomenon, to which a black swan was a matter of course – and, in truth, it was something very like it in that house. Mrs Cratchit made the gravy (ready beforehand in a little saucepan) hissing hot; Master Peter mashed the potatoes with incredible vigour; Miss Belinda sweetened up the apple sauce; Martha dusted the hot plates; Bob took Tiny Tim beside him in a tiny corner at the table; the two young Cratchits set chairs for everybody, not forgetting themselves, and, mounting guard upon their posts, crammed spoons into their mouths, lest they should shriek for goose before their turn came to be helped. At last the dishes were set on, and grace was said.

It was succeeded by a breathless pause, as Mrs Cratchit, looking slowly all along the carving-knife, prepared to plunge it in the breast; but when she did, and when the long-expected gush of stuffing issued forth, one murmur of delight arose all round the board, and even Tiny Tim, excited by the two young Cratchits, beat on the table with the handle of his knife, and feebly cried Hurrah!

There never was such a goose. Bob said he didn't believe there ever was such a goose cooked. Its tenderness and flavour, size and cheapness, were the themes of universal admiration. Eked out by apple sauce and mashed potatoes, it was sufficient dinner for the whole family; indeed, as Mrs Cratchit said with great delight (surveying one small atom of a bone upon the dish), they hadn't ate it all at last! Yet every one had had enough, and the youngest Cratchits, in particular, were steeped in sage and onion to the eyebrows! But now, the plates being changed by Miss Belinda, Mrs Cratchit left the room alone – too nervous to bear witnesses – to take the pudding up, and bring it in.

Suppose it should not be done enough! Suppose it should break in turning out! Suppose somebody should have got over the wall of the back yard, and stolen it, while they were merry with the goose – a supposition at which the two young Cratchits became livid! All sorts of horrors were supposed.

Hallo! A great deal of steam! The pudding was out of the copper. A smell like a washing-day! That was the cloth. A smell like an eating-house and a pastry-cook's next door to each other, with a laundress's next door to that! That was the pudding! In half a minute Mrs Cratchit entered – flushed, but smiling proudly – with the pudding, like a speckled cannonball, so hard and firm, blazing in half of half-a-quartern of ignited brandy, and bedight with Christmas holly stuck into the top.

Oh, a wonderful pudding! Bob Cratchit said, and calmly too, that he regarded it as the greatest success achieved by Mrs Cratchit since their marriage. Mrs Cratchit said that, now the weight was off her mind, she would confess she had her doubts about the quantity of flour. Everybody had something to say about it, but nobody said or thought it was at all a small pudding for a large family. It would have been flat heresy to do so. Any Cratchit would have blushed to hint at such a thing.

At last the dinner was all done, the cloth was cleared, the hearth swept, and the fire made up. The compound in the jug being tasted, and considered perfect, apples and oranges were put upon the table, and a shovel full of chestnuts on the fire. Then all the Cratchit family drew round the hearth in what Bob Cratchit called a circle, meaning half a one; and at Bob Cratchit's elbow stood the family display of glass – two tumblers, and a custard cup without a handle.

These held the hot stuff from the jug, however, as well as golden goblets would have done; and Bob served it out with beaming looks, while the chestnuts on the fire sputtered and crackled noisily. Then Bob proposed:

"A merry Christmas to us all, my dears. God bless us!"

Which all the family re-echoed.

"God bless us every one!" said Tiny Tim, the last of all.

Aunt Cyrilla's Christmas Basket

L. M. MONTGOMERY

Once again the true spirit of Christmas is represented as something homey and simple in this story from the Canadian author of Anne of Green Gables. First published in 1903 in Young People magazine, this story is about snobbish little Lucy Rose, a country girl who wants to be stylish and sophisticated. She's embarrassed by her no-nonsense Aunt Cyrilla and ashamed of the basketful of homemade treats that Aunt Cyrilla brings on a visit to their relatives. When the train becomes snowbound, even the wounded and despairing among the travelers are given new hope and inspiration by the kindness of a stranger.

When Lucy Rose met Aunt Cyrilla coming downstairs, somewhat flushed and breathless from her ascent to the garret, with a big, flat-covered basket hanging over her plump arm, she gave a little sigh of despair. Lucy Rose had done her brave best for some years – in fact, ever since she had put up her hair and lengthened her skirts – to break Aunt Cyrilla of the habit of carrying that basket with her every time she went to Pembroke; but Aunt Cyrilla still insisted on taking it, and only laughed at what she called Lucy Rose's "finicky notions". Lucy Rose had a horrible, haunting idea that it was extremely provincial for her aunt always to take the big basket, packed full of country good things, whenever she went to visit Edward and Geraldine. Geraldine was so stylish, and might think it queer; and then Aunt Cyrilla always would carry it on her arm and give cookies and apples and molasses taffy out of it to every child she encountered and, just as often as not, to older folks too. Lucy Rose, when she went to town with Aunt Cyrilla, felt chagrined over this – all of which goes to prove that Lucy was as yet very young and had a great deal to learn in this world.

That troublesome worry over what Geraldine would think nerved her to make a protest in this instance.

"Now, Aunt C'rilla," she pleaded, "you're surely not going to take that funny old basket to Pembroke this time – Christmas Day and all."

"'Deed and 'deed I am," returned Aunt Cyrilla briskly as she put it on the table and proceeded to dust it out. "I never went to see Edward and Geraldine since they were married that I didn't take a basket of good things along with me for them, and I'm not going to stop now. As for its being Christmas, all the more reason. Edward is always real glad to get some of the old farmhouse goodies. He says they beat city cooking all hollow, and so they do."

"But it's so countrified," moaned Lucy Rose.

"Well, I am countrified," said Aunt Cyrilla firmly, "and so are you. And what's more, I don't see that it's anything to be ashamed of. You've got some real silly pride about you, Lucy Rose. You'll grow out of it in time, but just now it is giving you a lot of trouble."

"The basket is a lot of trouble," said Lucy Rose crossly. "You're always mislaying it or afraid you will. And it does look so funny to be walking through the streets with that big, bulgy basket hanging on your arm."

"I'm not a mite worried about its looks," returned Aunt Cyrilla calmly. "As for its being a trouble, why, maybe it is, but I have that, and other people have the pleasure of it. Edward and Geraldine don't need it – I know that – but there may be those that will. And if it hurts your feelings to walk 'longside of a countrified old lady with a countrified basket, why, you can just fall behind, as it were."

Aunt Cyrilla nodded and smiled good-humouredly, and Lucy Rose, though she privately held to her own opinion, had to smile too.

"Now, let me see," said Aunt Cyrilla reflectively, tapping the snowy kitchen table with the point of her plump, dimpled forefinger, "what shall I take? That big fruitcake for one thing – Edward does like my fruitcake; and that cold boiled tongue for another. Those three mince pies too, they'd spoil before we got back or your uncle'd make himself sick eating them – mince pie is his besetting sin. And that little stone bottle full of cream – Geraldine may carry any amount of style, but I've yet to see her look down on real good country cream, Lucy Rose; and another bottle of my raspberry vinegar. That plate of jelly cookies and doughnuts will please the children and fill up the chinks, and you can bring me that box of ice-cream candy out of the pantry, and that bag of striped candy sticks your uncle brought home from the corner last night. And apples, of course – three or four dozen of those good eaters – and a little pot of my greengage preserves – Edward'll like that. And some sandwiches and pound cake for a snack for ourselves. Now, I guess that will do for eatables. The presents for the children can go in on top. There's a doll for Daisy and a little boat your uncle made for Ray and a tatted lace handkerchief apiece for the twins, and the crochet hood for the baby. Now, is that all?"

"There's a cold roast chicken in the pantry," said Lucy Rose wickedly, "and the pig Uncle Leo killed is hanging up in the porch. Couldn't you put them in too?"

Aunt Cyrilla smiled broadly. "Well, I guess we'll leave the pig alone; but since you have reminded me of it, the chicken may as well go in. I can make room."

Lucy Rose, in spite of her prejudices, helped with the packing and, not having been trained under Aunt Cyrilla's eye for nothing, did it very well too, with much clever economy of space. But when Aunt Cyrilla had put in as a finishing touch a big bouquet of pink and white everlastings, and tied the bulging covers down with a firm hand, Lucy Rose stood over the basket and whispered vindictively:

"Some day I'm going to burn this basket – when I get courage enough. Then there'll be an end of lugging it everywhere we go like a – like an old market-woman."

Uncle Leopold came in just then, shaking his head dubiously. He was not going to spend Christmas with Edward and Geraldine, and perhaps the prospect of having to cook and eat his Christmas dinner all alone made him pessimistic.

"I mistrust you folks won't get to Pembroke tomorrow," he said sagely. "It's going to storm."

Aunt Cyrilla did not worry over this. She believed matters of this kind were fore-ordained, and she slept calmly. But Lucy Rose got up three times in the night to see if it were storming, and when she did sleep, had horrible nightmares of struggling through blinding snowstorms dragging Aunt Cyrilla's Christmas basket along with her.

It was not snowing in the early morning, and Uncle Leopold drove Aunt Cyrilla and Lucy Rose and the basket to the station, four miles off. When they

reached there the air was thick with flying flakes. The stationmaster sold them their tickets with a grim face.

"If there's any more snow comes, the trains might as well keep Christmas too," he said. "There's been so much snow already that traffic is blocked half the time, and now there ain't no place to shovel the snow off onto."

Aunt Cyrilla said that if the train were to get to Pembroke in time for Christmas, it would get there; and she opened her basket and gave the stationmaster and three small boys an apple apiece.

"That's the beginning," groaned Lucy Rose to herself.

When their train came along, Aunt Cyrilla established herself in one seat and her basket in another, and looked beamingly around her at her fellow travellers.

These were few in number – a delicate little woman at the end of the car, with a baby and four other children, a young girl across the aisle with a pale, pretty face, a sunburned lad three seats ahead in a khaki uniform, a very handsome, imposing old lady in a sealskin coat ahead of him, and a thin young man with spectacles opposite.

"A minister," reflected Aunt Cyrilla, beginning to classify, "who takes better care of other folks' souls than of his own body; and that woman in the sealskin is discontented and cross at something – got up too early to catch the train, maybe; and that young chap must be one of the boys not long out of the hospital. That woman's children look as if they hadn't enjoyed a square meal since they were born; and if that girl across from me has a mother, I'd like to know what the woman means, letting her daughter go from home in this weather in clothes like that."

Lucy Rose merely wondered uncomfortably what the others thought of Aunt Cyrilla's basket.

They expected to reach Pembroke that night, but as the day wore on, the storm grew worse. Twice the train had to stop while the train hands dug it out. The third time it could not go on. It was dusk when the conductor came through the train, replying brusquely to the questions of the anxious passengers.

"A nice lookout for Christmas – no, impossible to go on or back – track blocked for miles – what's that, madam? – no, no station near – woods for miles. We're here for the night. These storms of late have played the mischief with everything."

"Oh, dear," groaned Lucy Rose.

Aunt Cyrilla looked at her basket complacently.

"At any rate, we won't starve," she said.

The pale, pretty girl seemed indifferent. The sealskin lady looked crosser than ever. The khaki boy said, "Just my luck," and two of the children began to cry. Aunt Cyrilla took some apples and striped candy sticks from her basket and carried them to them. She lifted the oldest into her ample lap and soon had them all around her, laughing and contented.

The rest of the travellers straggled over to the corner and drifted into conversation. The khaki boy said it was hard lines not to get home for Christmas, after all.

"I was invalided from South Africa three months ago, and I've been in the hospital at Netley ever since. Reached Halifax three days ago and telegraphed the old folks I'd eat my Christmas dinner with them, and to have an extra-big turkey because I didn't have any last year. They'll be badly disappointed."

He looked disappointed too. One khaki sleeve hung empty by his side. Aunt Cyrilla passed him an apple.

"We were all going down to Grandpa's for Christmas," said the little mother's oldest boy dolefully. "We've never been there before, and it's just too bad."

He looked as if he wanted to cry but thought better of it and bit off a mouthful of candy.

"Will there be any Santa Claus on the train?" demanded his small sister tearfully. "Jack says there won't."

"I guess he'll find you out," said Aunt Cyrilla reassuringly.

The pale, pretty girl came up and took the baby from the tired mother. "What a dear little fellow," she said softly.

"Are you going home for Christmas too?" asked Aunt Cyrilla.

The girl shook her head. "I haven't any home. I'm just a shop girl out of work at present, and I'm going to Pembroke to look for some."

Aunt Cyrilla went to her basket and took out her box of cream candy. "I guess we might as well enjoy ourselves. Let's eat it all up and have a good time. Maybe we'll get down to Pembroke in the morning."

The little group grew cheerful as they nibbled, and even the pale girl brightened up. The little mother told Aunt Cyrilla her story aside. She had been long estranged from her family, who had disapproved of her marriage. Her husband had died the previous summer, leaving her in poor circumstances.

"Father wrote to me last week and asked me to let bygones be bygones and come home for Christmas. I was so glad. And the children's hearts were set on it. It seems too bad that we are not to get there. I have to be back at work the morning after Christmas."

The khaki boy came up again and shared the candy. He told amusing stories of campaigning in South Africa. The minister came too, and listened, and even the sealskin lady turned her head over her shoulder.

By and by the children fell asleep, one on Aunt Cyrilla's lap and one on Lucy Rose's, and two on the seat. Aunt Cyrilla and the pale girl helped the mother make up beds for them. The minister gave his overcoat and the sealskin lady came forward with a shawl.

"This will do for the baby," she said.

"We must get up some Santa Claus for these youngsters," said the khaki boy. "Let's hang their stockings on the wall and fill 'em up as best we can. I've nothing about me but some hard cash and a jack-knife. I'll give each of 'em a quarter and the boy can have the knife."

"I've nothing but money either," said the sealskin lady regretfully. Aunt Cyrilla glanced at the little mother. She had fallen asleep with her head against the seat-back.

"I've got a basket over there," said Aunt Cyrilla firmly, "and I've some presents in it that I was taking to my nephew's children. I'm going to give 'em to these. As for the money, I think the mother is the one for it to go to. She's been telling me her story, and a pitiful one it is. Let's make up a little purse among us for a Christmas present."

The idea met with favour. The khaki boy passed his cap and everybody contributed. The sealskin lady put in a crumpled note. When Aunt Cyrilla straightened it out she saw that it was for twenty dollars.

Meanwhile, Lucy Rose had brought the basket. She smiled at Aunt Cyrilla as she lugged it down the aisle and Aunt Cyrilla smiled back. Lucy Rose had never touched that basket of her own accord before.

Ray's boat went to Jacky, and Daisy's doll to his older sister, the twins' lace handkerchiefs to the two smaller girls and the hood to the baby. Then the stockings were filled up with doughnuts and jelly cookies and the money was put in an envelope and pinned to the little mother's jacket.

"That baby is such a dear little fellow," said the sealskin lady gently. "He looks something like my little son. He died eighteen Christmases ago."

Aunt Cyrilla put her hand over the lady's kid glove. "So did mine," she said. Then the two women smiled tenderly at each other. Afterwards they rested from their labours and all had what Aunt Cyrilla called a "snack" of sandwiches and pound cake. The khaki boy said he hadn't tasted anything half so good since he left home.

"They didn't give us pound cake in South Africa," he said.

When the morning came the storm was still raging. The children wakened and went wild with delight over their stockings. The little mother found her envelope and tried to utter thanks and broke down; and nobody knew what to say or do, when the conductor fortunately came in and made a diversion by telling them they might as well resign themselves to spending Christmas on the train.

"This is serious," said the khaki boy, "when you consider that we've no provisions. Don't mind for myself, used to half rations or no rations at all. But these kiddies will have tremendous appetites."

Then Aunt Cyrilla rose to the occasion.

"I've got some emergency rations here," she announced. "There's plenty for all and we'll have our Christmas dinner, although a cold one. Breakfast first thing. There's a sandwich apiece left and we must fill up on what is left of the cookies and doughnuts and save the rest for a real good spread at dinnertime. The only thing is, I haven't any bread."

"I've a box of soda crackers," said the little mother eagerly.

Nobody in that car will ever forget that Christmas. To begin with, after breakfast they had a concert. The khaki boy gave two recitations, sang three songs, and gave a whistling solo. Lucy Rose gave three recitations and the minister a comic reading. The pale shop girl sang two songs. It was agreed that the khaki boy's whistling solo was the best number, and Aunt Cyrilla gave him the bouquet of everlastings as a reward of merit.

Then the conductor came in with the cheerful news that the storm was almost over and he thought the track would be cleared in a few hours.

"If we can get to the next station we'll be all right," he said. "The branch joins the main line there and the tracks will be clear."

At noon they had dinner. The train hands were invited in to share it. The minister carved the chicken with the brakeman's jack-knife and the khaki boy cut up the tongue and the mince pies, while the sealskin lady mixed the raspberry vinegar with its due proportion of water. Bits of paper served as plates. The train furnished a couple of glasses, a tin pint cup was discovered and given to the children, Aunt Cyrilla and Lucy Rose and the sealskin lady drank, turn about, from the latter's graduated medicine glass, the shop girl and the little mother shared one of the empty bottles and the khaki boy, the minister and the train men drank out of the other bottle.

Everybody declared they had never enjoyed a meal more in their lives. Certainly it was a merry one, and Aunt Cyrilla's cooking was never more appreciated; indeed, the bones of the chicken and the pot of preserves were all that was left. They could not eat the preserves because they had no spoons, so Aunt Cyrilla gave them to the little mother.

When all was over, a hearty vote of thanks was passed to Aunt Cyrilla

and her basket. The sealskin lady wanted to know how she made her pound cake, and the khaki boy asked for her recipe for jelly cookies. And when two hours later the conductor came in and said the snowploughs had got along and they'd soon be starting, they all wondered if it could really be less than twenty-four hours since they met.

"I feel as if I'd been campaigning with you all my life," said the khaki boy.

At the next station they all parted. The little mother and the children had to take the next train back home. The minister stayed there, and the khaki boy and the sealskin lady changed trains. The sealskin lady shook Aunt Cyrilla's hand. She no longer looked discontented or cross.

"This has been the pleasantest Christmas I have ever spent," she said heartily. "I shall never forget that wonderful basket of yours. The little shop girl is going home with me. I've promised her a place in my husband's store."

When Aunt Cyrilla and Lucy Rose reached Pembroke there was nobody there to meet them because everyone had given up expecting them. It was not far from the station to walk to Edward's house and Aunt Cyrilla elected to walk.

"I'll carry the basket," said Lucy Rose.

Aunt Cyrilla relinquished it with a smile. Lucy Rose smiled too.

"It's a blessed old basket," said the latter, "and I love it. Please forget all the silly things I ever said about it, Aunt C'rilla."

Christmas at Mole End

KENNETH GRAHAME

Here's another great family favorite, taken from Kenneth Grahame's classic, The Wind in the Willows. When the field mice come caroling to Mole's house, he and Ratty have a perfect excuse for a party. As a heartwarming picture of neighbors enjoying each other's company, sharing good food and drink, and making their own fun, this is impossible to beat! Mole and Ratty remind me of two slightly shabby Edwardian gents with their preference for sardines and German sausage. The chilly little mice seem pleased to be bossed around so that they can share a warm welcome and some lively entertainment.

"What a capital little house this is!" Mr Rat called out cheerily. "So compact! So well planned! Everything here and everything in its place! We'll make a jolly night of it. The first thing we want is a good fire; I'll see to that – I always know where to find things. So this is the parlour? Splendid! Your own idea, those little sleeping-bunks in the wall? Capital! Now, I'll fetch the wood and the coals, and you get a duster, Mole – you'll find one in the drawer of the kitchen table – and try and smarten things up a bit. Bustle about, old chap!"

Encouraged by his inspiriting companion, the Mole roused himself and dusted and polished with energy and heartiness, while the Rat, running to and fro with armfuls of fuel, soon had a cheerful blaze roaring up the chimney. He hailed the Mole to come and warm himself; but Mole promptly had another fit of the blues, dropping down on a couch in dark despair and burying his face in his duster. "Rat," he moaned, "how about your supper, you poor, cold, hungry, weary animal? I've nothing to give you – nothing – not a crumb!"

"What a fellow you are for giving in!" said the Rat reproachfully. "Why, only just now I saw a sardine-opener on the kitchen dresser, quite distinctly; and everybody knows that means there are sardines about somewhere in the neighbourhood. Rouse yourself! Pull yourself together, and come with me and forage."

They went and foraged accordingly, hunting through every cupboard and turning out every drawer. The result was not so very depressing after all, though of course it might have been better; a tin of sardines – a box of captain's biscuits, nearly full – and a German sausage encased in silver paper.

"There's a banquet for you!" observed the Rat, as he arranged the table. "I know some animals who would give their ears to be sitting down to supper with us tonight!"

"No bread!" groaned the Mole dolorously; "no butter, no – "

"No pâté de foie gras, no champagne!" continued the Rat, grinning. "And that reminds me – what's that little door at the end of the passage? Your cellar, of course! Every luxury in this house! Just you wait a minute."

He made for the cellar door, and presently reappeared, somewhat dusty, with a bottle of beer in each paw and another under each arm. "Self-indulgent beggar you seem to be, Mole," he observed. "Deny yourself nothing. This is really the jolliest little place I ever was in. Now, wherever did you pick up those prints? Make the place look so home-like, they do. No wonder you're so fond of it, Mole. Tell us all about it, and how you came to make it what it is."

Then, while the Rat busied himself fetching plates, and knives and forks, and mustard which he mixed in an egg-cup, the Mole, his bosom still heaving with the stress of his recent emotion, related – somewhat shyly at first, but with more freedom as he warmed to his subject – how this was planned, and how that was thought out, and how this was got through a windfall from an aunt, and that was a wonderful find and a bargain, and this other thing was bought out of laborious savings and a certain amount of "going without". His spirits finally quite restored, he must needs go and caress his possessions, and take a lamp and show off their points to his visitor and expatiate on them, quite forgetful of the supper they both so much needed; Rat, who was desperately hungry but strove to conceal it, nodding seriously, examining with a puckered brow, and saying, "wonderful" and "most remarkable" at intervals, when the chance for an observation was given him.

At last the Rat succeeded in decoying him to the table, and had just got seriously to work with the sardine-opener when sounds were heard from the forecourt without – sounds like the scuffling of small feet in the gravel and a confused murmur of tiny voices, while broken sentences reached them – "Now, all in a line – hold the lantern up a bit, Tommy – clear your throats first – no coughing after I say one, two, three. – Where's young Bill? – Here, come on, do, we're all a-waiting – "

"What's up?" inquired the Rat, pausing in his labours.

"I think it must be the field-mice," replied the Mole, with a touch of pride in his manner. "They go round carol-singing regularly at this time of the year. They're quite an institution in these parts. And they never pass me over – they come to Mole End last of all; and I used to give them hot drinks, and supper sometimes, when I could afford it. It will be like old times to hear them again."

"Let's have a look!" cried the Rat, jumping up and running to the door.

It was a pretty sight, and a seasonable one, that met their eyes when they flung the door open. In the forecourt, lit by the dim rays of a horn lantern, some eight or ten little field-mice stood in a semicircle, red worsted comforters round their throats, their forepaws thrust deep into their pockets, their feet jigging for warmth. With bright beady eyes they glanced shyly at each other, sniggering a little, sniffing and applying coat-sleeves a good deal. As the door opened, one of the elder ones that carried the lantern was just saying, "Now then, one, two, three!" and forthwith their shrill little voices uprose on the air, singing one of the old-time carols that their forefathers composed in fields that were fallow and held by frost, or when snow-bound in chimney corners, and handed down to be sung in the miry street to lamp-lit windows at Yule-time. The voices ceased, the singers, bashful but smiling, exchanged sidelong glances, and silence succeeded – but for a moment only.

Then, from up above and far away, down the tunnel they had so lately travelled, was borne to their ears in a faint musical hum the sound of distant bells ringing a joyful and clangorous peal.

"Very well sung, boys!" cried the Rat heartily. "And now come along in, all of you, and warm yourselves by the fire, and have something hot!"

"Yes, come along, field-mice," cried the Mole eagerly. "This is quite like old times! Shut the door after you. Pull up that settle to the fire. Now, you just wait a minute, while we – O, Ratty!" he cried in despair, plumping down on a seat, with tears impending. "Whatever are we doing? We've nothing to give them!"

"You leave all that to me," said the masterful Rat. "Here, you with the lantern! Come over this way. I want to talk to you. Now, tell me, are there any shops open at this hour of the night?"

"Why, certainly, sir," replied the field-mouse respectfully. "At this time of the year our shops keep open to all sorts of hours."

"Then look here!" said the Rat. "You go off at once, you and your lantern, and you get me – "

Here much muttered conversation ensued, and the Mole only heard bits of it, such as – "Fresh, mind! – no, a pound of that will do – see you get Buggins's, for I won't have any other – no, only the best – if you can't get it there, try somewhere else – yes, of course, home-made, no tinned stuff – well then, do the best you can!" Finally, there was a chink of coin passing from paw to paw, the field-mouse was provided with an ample basket for his purchases, and off he hurried, he and his lantern.

The rest of the field-mice, perched in a row on the settle, their small legs swinging, gave themselves up to enjoyment of the fire, and toasted their chilblains till they tingled; while the Mole, failing to draw them into easy conversation, plunged into family history and made each of them recite the names of his numerous brothers, who were too young, it appeared, to be allowed to go out a-carolling this year, but looked forward very shortly to winning the parental consent.

The Rat, meanwhile, was busy examining the label on one of the beer-bottles. "I perceive this to be Old Burton," he remarked approvingly. "Sensible Mole! The very thing! Now we shall be able to mull some ale! Get the things ready, Mole, while I draw the corks."

It did not take long to prepare the brew and thrust the tin heater well into the red heart of the fire; and soon every field-mouse was sipping and coughing and choking (for a little mulled ale goes a long way) and wiping his eyes and laughing and forgetting he had ever been cold in all his life.

"They act plays too, these fellows," the Mole explained to the Rat. "Make them up all by themselves, and act them afterwards. And very well they do it, too! They gave us a capital one last year, about a field-mouse who was captured at sea by a Barbary corsair, and made to row in a galley; and when he escaped and got home again, his lady-love had gone into a convent. Here, you! You were in it, I remember. Get up and recite a bit."

The field-mouse addressed got up on his legs, giggled shyly, looked round the room, and remained absolutely tongue-tied. His comrades cheered him on, Mole coaxed and encouraged him, and the Rat went so far as to take him by the shoulders and shake him; but nothing could overcome his stage-fright. They were all busily engaged on him like watermen applying the Royal Humane Society's regulations to a case of long submersion, when the latch clicked, the door opened, and the field-mouse with the lantern reappeared, staggering under the weight of his basket.

There was no more talk of play-acting once the very real and solid contents of the basket had been tumbled out on the table. Under the generalship of Rat, everybody was set to do something or to fetch something. In a very few minutes supper was ready, and Mole, as he took the head of the table in a sort of a dream, saw a lately barren board set thick with savoury comforts; saw his little friends' faces brighten and beam as they fell to without delay; and then let himself loose – for he was famished indeed – on the provender so magically provided, thinking what a happy home-coming this had turned out, after all. As they ate, they talked of old times, and the field-mice gave him the local gossip up to date, and answered as well as they could the hundred questions he had to ask them. The Rat said little or nothing, only taking care that each guest had what he wanted, and plenty of it, and that Mole had no trouble or anxiety about anything.

They clattered off at last, very grateful and showering wishes of the season, with their jacket pockets stuffed with remembrances for the small brothers and sisters at home. When the door had closed on the last of them and the chink of the lanterns had died away, Mole and Rat kicked the fire up, drew their chairs in, brewed themselves a last nightcap of mulled ale, and discussed the events of the long day. At last the Rat, with a tremendous yawn, said, "Mole, old chap, I'm ready to drop. Sleepy is simply not the word. That your own bunk over on that side? Very well, then, I'll take this. What a ripping little house this is! Everything so handy!"

He clambered into his bunk and rolled himself well up in the blankets, and slumber gathered him forthwith, as a swathe of barley is folded into the arms of the reaping machine.

The weary Mole also was glad to turn in without delay, and soon had his head on his pillow, in great joy and contentment.

A Gift from the Heart

SAVIOUR PIROTTA

When I was a boy, poinsettias survived on shelves and windowsills in our house long after the cacti and camellias and African violets had been killed by kindness—too much water, too much plant food. So I always thought of them as being sturdy but a little bit boring. However, since coming across this story I've learned to be much more respectful! According to a Mexican legend, the poinsettia was once a humble weed, but by a miracle, it became as beautiful as the star that shone over the stable at Bethlehem. And why the miracle? Because it was given with love by someone who had nothing else to give.

Once there was a Mexican girl whose father was a fisherman. She was named Maria Flores, after her mother who'd died when the girl was still a baby.

One night during supper Maria's father said, "My fishing nets have been empty for weeks, little one. We can't go on like this, not being able to pay our debts. I've found work on a ship sailing to Europe. You'll have to spend the winter with your *abuela* in her village, San Domingo."

"But that means we won't be together for Christmas," cried Maria. "We always spend Christmas together."

Papa gave her a big hug. "Sometimes we have to do things we find hard, little one. It's all been arranged; your grandma's expecting you. If you leave tomorrow, you'll be there by Christmas."

"I understand," said Maria. "Perhaps we'll spend Christmas together next year."

Her father gave her another hug and then stood up and fetched the money tin from its hiding place behind the stove. "We'll have to buy some presents, of course. You can't go empty-handed."

Maria agreed. No one she knew would ever visit a friend or a relative without taking a gift of some kind. The next day she helped Papa choose suitable presents at the market. They had very little money, but they managed to get a shawl for Grandma and cotton handkerchiefs for all her relatives.

The shopping done, and her clothes packed in a neat bundle, Maria kissed her father goodbye and set off for her grandma's village, a remote hamlet in the mountains. The holidays had already started, and lots of other people were traveling too, hoping to get home in time for a good Christmas dinner.

Her father had booked her a seat on a horse-drawn cart, which took her all the way to the foot of the sierra. Beyond that, the path up the mountain was too steep for the cart. Maria continued her journey on a mule, with the San Domingo pharmacist who'd come down the mountain to buy medicine.

It was late at night, and Maria had fallen asleep on her mule, when they finally reached Grandma's village.

"Wake up," said the pharmacist. "We're almost home."

Maria rubbed the sleep from her eyes and saw lights flickering ahead. They reminded her of the lanterns her papa and the other fishermen put on their boats.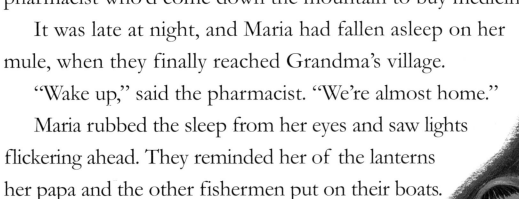

"Your relatives are waiting for you," said the pharmacist.

The mule stopped under a tree, where several people were huddled together against the cold, the grown-ups holding lamps. No one spoke until an old woman stepped forward and said in a very loud voice, "Welcome to our village, Maria Flores. I am your *abuela.*"

She kissed Maria loudly on each cheek and then all the others crowded around her, hugging her and shaking her hand.

"How was your journey?"

"You must be tired and hungry."

"I am your cousin. I went to school with your mother, God rest her soul."

Maria felt like a princess in a fairy tale as she was swept into Grandma's house, where a feast of cakes and hot chocolate had been laid out on the table. It seemed as if the whole village had gathered in Grandma's kitchen, eager to see the visitor.

"Isn't she a beautiful child?"

"The spitting image of her mother."

"And so tall for her age, too."

Later, lying in a warm cot by the stove and feeling sleepy from too much travel and too much hot chocolate, Maria thought how lucky she was. She'd never met

any of her mother's relatives before, but they had all come to welcome her.

"I'm glad I brought them all a present," she said to herself. "It'll show them that I love them, too."

The next day was Christmas Eve. After a special Christmas supper during which they exchanged presents, the people of San Domingo got ready to go to church.

"It's time for Baby Jesus to get his presents," said Grandma.

"What do you mean?" asked Maria.

"We have a statue of Baby Jesus in the church," explained Grandma. "Every year we place gifts at its feet. It's an old local custom."

"But I haven't got anything to give Jesus," said Maria.

"It doesn't matter," said Grandma. "You are a visitor. No one will speak ill of you."

"But I can't go to church empty-handed," said Maria. "It would be rude."

"I'm taking a basket of almonds," said Grandma. "Why don't we share them? I have a pretty box you could put them in."

"That's very kind of you, *Abuela*," said Maria, "but my gift has to come from me."

She racked her brains, trying to think what she could give Jesus.

"Perhaps I can pick some flowers," she said. "Jesus would like some flowers."

"Yes," said Grandma, "that would be a fine present."

There was a piece of land behind Grandma's house where the soil was too stony for farming. Maria was sure she'd find some flowers there—wild daisies perhaps or mountain roses. Alas, she could find none. The field had been picked clean by people who wanted to decorate their Christmas tables. Maria could see nothing but weeds. *What a stingy gift for the King of Heaven and Earth,* she thought sadly. But there wasn't time to try and find something else.

The church bells were summoning everyone to the midnight celebration; Grandma was calling from the kitchen window. Maria picked a handful of the weeds, choosing the leafiest, and carried them inside. Grandma wrapped them up carefully in a silk shawl, as if they were a bouquet of fragrant blooms.

In church a choir started to sing carols as people approached the altar where the statue of Baby Jesus lay in a manger, a small crown on its head. One by one they placed gifts at its feet. A few who were rich gave items of jewelry or pots of expensive perfume. But most had brought humbler gifts: eggs laid by their own hens, nuts and fruits gathered in the harvest, or little fruitcakes baked in outside ovens. The people in the village did not have much money to spare.

Soon it was Maria's turn to give Jesus her gift. Grandma nudged her gently, and they stood up together. All eyes were on them as they slowly advanced down the aisle. Maria heard people whispering.

"What's the old woman's gift?"

"Almonds in a basket."

"And what has the girl got under that silk shawl?"

"Flowers, by the looks of it. They must be very fragile to be covered like that."

Just wait until they realize I've only got weeds, thought Maria. *They'll think I want to insult Jesus, not give him a present.*

She had a sudden urge to turn and run away. She could keep on running until she'd left the church and the village behind. Then she remembered what her papa had said to her only a few days before.

"Sometimes we have to do things we find hard, little one."

Well, it was very hard for Maria to keep on walking down that aisle with a bunch of weeds in her hands. But, she firmly told herself, her gift was for Jesus, not for the people of San Domingo to admire. As long as Jesus liked it she didn't care what other people said.

Before she knew it, Maria was at the altar. She saw Grandma kneel and place her basket of almonds in front of the statue. She knelt to put her bouquet among the other gifts.

Just then one of the men in the front pews leaned forward. "Take off the shawl, dear," he whispered. "Show the people what lovely flowers you're giving Jesus."

"I can't," Maria whispered back.

The man smiled, thinking Maria couldn't undo the silk shawl. He took the bunch from her, saying, "Here, I'll do it for you."

Gently, he pulled away the cloth. The people in the church gasped.

"What wonderful flowers."

"Beautiful."

"I've never seen anything like them in all my life."

Maria stared. The weeds weren't weeds anymore. They had changed into flowers shaped like Christmas stars. The green leaves at the top had grown bigger and turned into red, velvety petals.

Speechless, Maria realized that Jesus had worked a miracle. He'd seen the beauty of her gift, which came from the heart, and decided to share it with everyone in the church.

No one in the congregation guessed what had just happened. Everyone assumed that Maria had bought the gorgeous flowers on her way to the village.

The little girl did not tell anyone about the miracle either. She knew no one would believe her anyway. Only her grandma, who'd seen what happened, shared her secret. After Christmas the old woman planted the flowers in the bit of land where Maria had picked the weeds. They grew into a large bush that flowered every year in December. Today this flower is called the poinsettia, and it grows in many countries around the world. People take huge bunches of it to church every Christmas to show Jesus how much they love him.

Just like Maria Flores did all those years ago in Mexico!

The Legend of St. Nicholas

ANN PILLING

In some countries, such as the Netherlands and Germany, it's not Santa Claus who delivers Christmas presents but St. Nicholas. St. Nicholas was a real person—a bishop of the church who lived in what is now Turkey in the A.D. 300s. A deeply devout man, he became the patron saint of children, and his feast day is celebrated on December 6th. Have you ever asked yourself—Why does Santa Claus come down the chimney? Why don't we ever catch a glimpse of him? And why do we get presents in stockings? This story by Ann Pilling has the answers!

Long, long ago there was a very rich man who had three beautiful daughters. The man wanted these daughters to marry good husbands, who would take care of them and make sure they lived in comfort all through their lives. But he had to give the husbands dowries—a bag full of money, one for each daughter.

The man was a merchant, and he was rich because he owned ships that sailed the seas, bringing back jewels and gold and carpets, peacocks and elephants' tusks. These he sold for more money than his sailors had paid for them. Everyone wanted to buy the things that were brought home in his fine tall ships.

But one day a terrible thing happened. A great storm blew just as his ships were close to the shore. They were thrown onto the rocks and sank to the bottom of the sea, and the merchant's treasures were lost forever.

He was now very poor. He had to sell his fine big house and move into a tiny cottage with his daughters. They lived on nothing but bread and soup, and there were no servants to take care of them. Every day the girls washed their long stockings (they only had one pair each) and hung them up to dry by the fire.

"What about our marriage dowries?" they asked their father. "Nobody will marry us now. What will happen to us?"

The merchant said nothing. He did not want to tell his daughters that they might have to go and be servants. He had no money left at all to help them.

One cold winter's night, just before Christmas, the poor man and his three daughters had gone to bed as usual but not before the daughters had hung up their stockings to dry over the fire. A stranger came creeping along the street in the shadows. He was wearing a long, red robe, right down to his toes, and a tall, pointed hat. He peeped into the cottage window and then tried to open it, but it was stuck. Climbing up onto the roof, he stuffed something down the chimney. Then he went silently away.

In the morning the oldest daughter, whose name was Gerda, found that one of her stockings was fat and bulging. When she turned it inside out, she found a bag full of gold coins! Her father used the money for her dowry, and soon she was married to a man she greatly loved. But nobody knew where the gold had come from, even though the family asked everyone they met.

Just one year later the second daughter, who was named Anna, sat weeping by the fire. It was time for her wedding, but there was no money for her dowry. She went to bed early that night and cried herself to sleep as the snow fell outside her window, leaving the silent town all white and gleaming.

In the morning it was exactly as before. Her stocking was full of gold, and the merchant was able to give it as a dowry to the handsome young man who wanted to marry her. So a second wedding took place, and Anna was filled with happiness. Once again the merchant asked everybody if they knew who might have come during the night and filled Anna's stocking with gold, but again nobody could tell him.

Now only little Kristina was left. Gentle Hans wanted to marry her very much, but she had no dowry, and without that they would be very poor. It was too much to hope that the mysterious giver of the gold would come a third time. Exactly one year after Anna's wedding, Kristina said her prayers one snowy night, hoping that something wonderful might happen to her as it had to her sisters. Then she climbed into bed and fell asleep.

But her father was awake.
He was hiding in the shadows
down in the kitchen, where the fire
burned low and where Kristina's
stockings were hanging on a string
to dry. And just as the church clock
struck midnight, he heard a muffled
bumpity-bump sound up in the
chimney and watched as something
big and dark and round fell out of
the sooty darkness and landed in
the mouth of one of the stockings.
It was another bag of gold!

The merchant opened his door and went into the street. "Wait!" he called out to the dark figure that was hurrying away. "Who are you, and why have you been so kind to us? At least tell me your name so that I may say thank you."

But the man shook his head. "Nobody must know my name," he replied, "and I don't want any thanks. Go in peace and may the Lord bless you this Christmas."

The stranger's name was Nicholas. He too had once been a rich merchant, but now he was a bishop of the church. He had heard what had happened to the merchant's family and wanted to help. Nicholas was such a good man that when he died he was made into a saint, and people still say prayers to him asking for his help when they are in trouble. In the Netherlands and Belgium—and in Austria and Germany too—St. Nicholas comes on his own special day, December 6th, to reward the children for being good. In other countries he comes on Christmas Eve to deliver children's presents down the chimney. And there's another thing. If you say "St. Nicholas" fast and in a sleepy kind of voice, it sounds a bit like Santa Claus . . .

Befana and the Three Wise Men

VIVIAN FRENCH

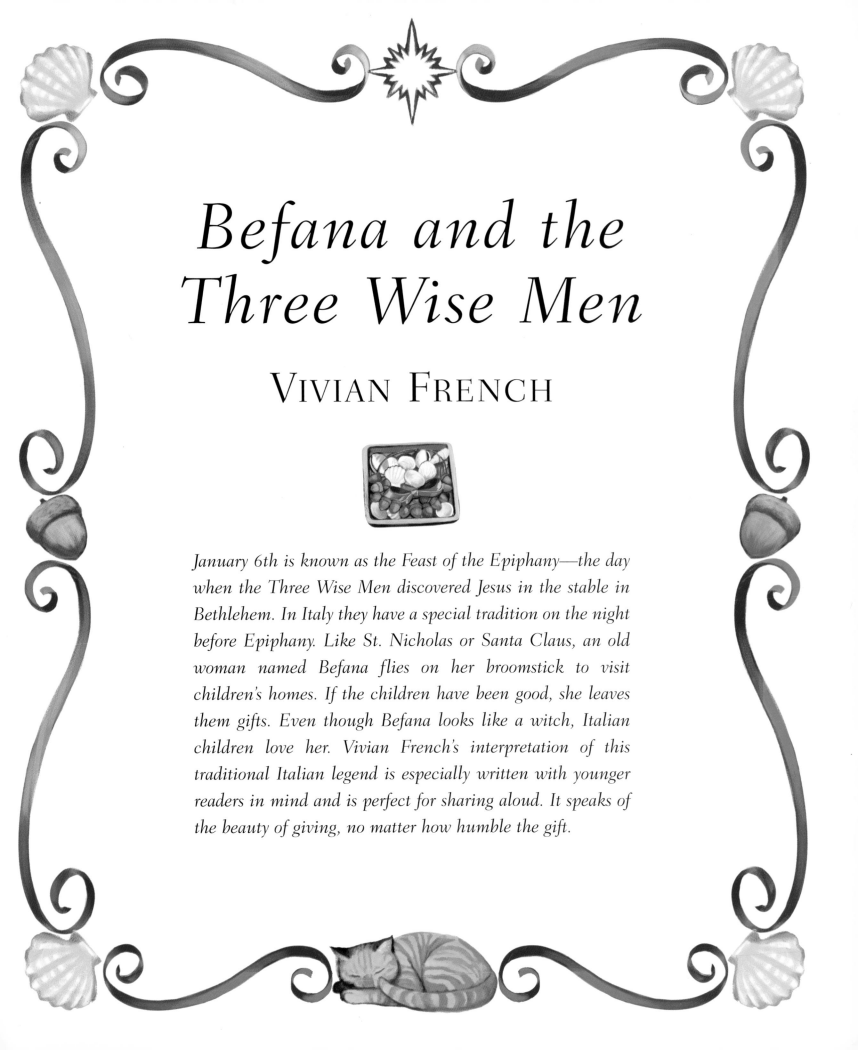

January 6th is known as the Feast of the Epiphany—the day when the Three Wise Men discovered Jesus in the stable in Bethlehem. In Italy they have a special tradition on the night before Epiphany. Like St. Nicholas or Santa Claus, an old woman named Befana flies on her broomstick to visit children's homes. If the children have been good, she leaves them gifts. Even though Befana looks like a witch, Italian children love her. Vivian French's interpretation of this traditional Italian legend is especially written with younger readers in mind and is perfect for sharing aloud. It speaks of the beauty of giving, no matter how humble the gift.

The big tabby cat was lying on the roof, keeping out of the way of the sweeping and cleaning going on below . . . not that there was ever a speck of dirt to be seen in Befana's tiny tumbledown cottage. Tabby listened to the steady *swish! swish! swish!* of Befana's broom and yawned. The last

rays of the sun were warming his thick fur, and he was sleepy, but he was keeping one eye on a small, bright star. It shone steadily over the hills to the east, and Tabby was certain he had never seen it before.

Jingle! Jingle! Pad . . . pad . . . pad . . . pad . . .

Tabby turned his head. There was a narrow track leading to the cottage, but it was overgrown and hardly ever used. Befana, old and crotchety as she was, had no friends. Tabby stretched and stood up to see who could be visiting them.

"*SSSSSST!*" His fur stood up straight on end. Three tall men were riding one behind the other; three tall men dressed in silks and satins, that was odd enough—but what were the strange humpbacked creatures that they were riding on? Tabby slithered his way down the roof and shot through the open kitchen door with a loud *MERROW!!!!*

The bent old woman sweeping the bare stone floor looked up in surprise. "Tabby? What is it?"

Tabby stayed under the table.

Befana tucked the broom firmly under her arm. "Don't you fret, Tabby,"

she said. "I'll deal with it!" And she hurried out
of the door.

CRASH! The broom fell as Befana stared and
stared. Inside the kitchen Tabby backed under
a cupboard, his whiskers quivering. Beyond the
dilapidated fence three camels looked down
their long noses.

"Hunh!" they snorted. "Hunh!"

The tallest stranger spoke sharply in
a language Befana did not understand.
At once the camels lowered themselves
heavily to the ground. The three
lords—Befana was certain they
must be lords—climbed off the
kneeling animals and walked
toward her.

Befana sank down into a
curtsy, but she picked up
her broom as she rose.

"There is no need to fear us," said the tallest man. "We mean you no harm."

"We have lost our way," said the second. "All we ask is shelter for the night."

"And perhaps—" the third man glanced at the small row of withered onions in the garden. "Perhaps—a drink of water?"

Befana looked hard at the strangers. She saw the dark shadows under their eyes, and she saw that their silks were <u>faded</u> and their satins torn. Most of all, she could see that all three were weary to the bone.

"You can come inside," she told them. "And there'll be something to eat."

Under the cupboard Tabby growled quietly. He knew how little food there was in the cottage; hardly enough for one old woman and her cat, let alone three strange men and their peculiar beasts. He watched as Befana chopped up an onion and sliced the two small potatoes meant for supper, and he narrowed his big yellow eyes. The soup would be very thin indeed tonight.

If the three visitors agreed with Tabby, they did not say so. They ate their soup slowly and carefully, making sure no drop was wasted. Then the tallest man stood up and bowed to Befana.

"We thank you for your food and kindness," he said. "I am Caspar, and my two companions are Melchior and Balthasar. For many years we have studied the stars, and we know that now is the time when a new king is to be born . . . a king who will be greater than any that has ever been. We are traveling east to greet him and bring him gifts." Befana nodded and began tidying away the wooden bowls. Tabby noticed she had eaten nothing herself and that there was nothing for a hungry cat except onion skins.

"The great king's birthplace is marked by a star," Melchior said. "It hangs in the sky both day and night, but today the skies were cloudy, and we lost our way."

Befana nodded once more and began to lay out thin and much-mended blankets for the three men to sleep on. Tabby, seeing that they were from Befana's own bed, sighed. With a twirl of his tail, he slipped away from under the cupboard and went to find a comfortable place of his own to sleep . . . and a nice fat mouse for his supper.

Balthasar looked at Befana and smiled. "Why don't you come with us?" he asked. "You could be among the first to greet the greatest king in all the world."

Befana smoothed the last blanket into place. "A king would have no time for the likes of me," she said. "What do I know about kings? And, besides, how could I leave my cottage?"

"This king is only a newborn baby," Balthasar said gently. "And we believe he may be somewhere poor and humble. It may not be a palace that we search for . . . it could perhaps be a cottage such as yours or even a stable."

Befana frowned. "But you have presents to give this king."

"Indeed," Caspar said. "We bring him gold, frankincense, and myrrh."

"But he does not need gifts," Balthasar said quickly. "A little baby knows nothing about gold or precious spices. What a baby needs is love. The love of someone who would give up even their own blankets to keep a stranger warm."

Befana paused for a moment and then shook her head. "No," she said. "No. There's too much here for me to do. Just think of the dirt that would come creeping in if I wasn't here to sweep it away!" And she handed Balthasar her guttering candle and went off to her attic and her cold, blanketless bed.

Befana got up early the next morning, but her visitors were up even earlier. The camels were saddled and ready, and Caspar and Melchior were standing by the open door. The star was shining brightly in the pale dawn sky.

Balthasar moved away from the hearth, and Befana saw that he had piled logs by the grate and lit the fire for her. Tabby was sitting, gazing at the flames and purring loudly.

"Thank you," Befana said gruffly.

Balthasar smiled. "It was nothing," he said. "And I ask you again—won't you come with us to see the baby king?"

The old woman looked around her room. The blankets were neatly folded, but they weren't where they should be. She could see dusty footprints on the floor, and the soup bowls were still waiting to be washed.

"No," she said slowly. "No . . . but I wish him well."

Tabby stood up and stretched. He stared at Befana with his big yellow eyes. "Merrow," he said. "Merrow!" And he walked purposefully toward the door.

Balthasar laughed. "See?" he said. "See? Even your cat is telling you to come with us!"

But Befana turned her back and began to shake out the blankets. Balthasar lifted his hand in farewell and walked away to where his camel was waiting.

Befana fetched water from the well and scoured the bowls. She took the blankets back to her attic. She swept the floor and scrubbed it fiercely. She only noticed that Tabby was missing when she called him at lunchtime.

"Tabby! Tabby!"

There was no answer.

Befana called and called and looked high and low, but the big tabby was nowhere to be found. She sank onto a chair.

"What kind of a king can this be?" she said to herself. "What kind of a king that a star would shine down on his place of birth? What kind of a baby that even my cat runs away to see him?"

And she sat very still, thinking.

Suddenly, she jumped to her feet. "I WILL go," she said. "I WILL see this baby king!" She ran to the cupboard and opened it. Inside was a box of shells, a worn blue ribbon, and a necklace of acorns.

"Presents!" she said happily. "Presents for a baby!"

She snatched up her gifts and marched out of her door. Down the path and through the gate she hurried, calling, "Wait! Wait! I'm coming with you . . . I'm coming to see the baby king!"

But there was no answer. The three wise men and Tabby were far along the road, always moving farther and farther away. On Befana ran, on and on . . .

And on and on and on she runs, still looking, still hoping. If she passes a house where there are children, she leaves a gift, because—who knows? Maybe one day she'll find that special baby, and he'll smile at her and hold out his arms . . .

The *Fir Tree*

HANS CHRISTIAN ANDERSEN

When you think of Christmas, you probably picture a Christmas tree. In most places where Christmas is celebrated the tree is very important. The evergreen branches symbolize new life. This custom comes from Germany and Scandinavia, where traditional decorations include glass ornaments, nuts, cakes, and small gifts. German immigrants brought the tradition to the United States in the 1700s, but it wasn't until the mid-1800s that trees became an essential part of Christmas. Jenny Koralek's retelling of this fairy tale by Hans Christian Andersen is melancholy, but I like it for the intensity of its feeling; it's full of the yearning and sadness we feel as the party comes to an end. Save it to read once the decorations have been taken down, when Christmas is over for another year . . .

Out in the forest stood a pretty little Fir Tree. It grew in a good place where there was plenty of sunlight and air. It was surrounded by many larger trees—pines as well as firs—but the little Fir Tree longed to grow bigger. It took no notice of the warm sun and the fresh air or of the children who came chattering into the forest to look for strawberries and raspberries. Often they passed by with a basketful and would sit down by the little Fir Tree and say, "How pretty that small one is!" But that was not at all what the tree wanted to hear.

During the next year it had grown a new shoot, and the following year it grew even taller. You can always tell how many years a tree has been growing by the number of rings it has in its trunk.

"Oh, if only I were as big as the others!" sighed the little Fir Tree. "Then I would spread my branches far around and look out onto the wide world from my top. The birds would build nests in my branches, and when the wind blew, I would nod just as proudly as the other trees."

In the winter, when the snow lay all around, white and sparkling, a hare came jumping along and leaped right over the little Fir Tree, which made it very angry. But when three winters had gone by, the little tree had grown so tall that the hare had to run around it.

Oh, to grow and to grow and be old! Surely that's the best thing in the world, thought the tree.

In the fall woodcutters always came and chopped down some of the largest trees. The little Fir Tree shuddered with fear, for the great trees fell to the ground with a crash, and their branches were cut off so that the trees looked quite bare. They were laid on wagons and dragged away. *Where were they going?* the little Fir Tree wondered.

In the spring, when the swallows and the stork came, the tree asked them, "Do you know where the trees go? Have you seen them?"

The swallows said, "No," but the stork said: "Yes, I think so. I saw many new ships when I flew out of Egypt. They had very tall masts; I think that those were the trees. They smelled like fir. All I can say is that they were tall and stately—very stately."

"I wish I was big enough to go over the sea!" sighed the little Fir Tree. "What kind of thing is this sea, and what does it look like?"

"It would take too long to explain all that," said the stork, and he went away.

"Be happy that you are still young and strong," said the sunbeams.

And the wind and the rain kissed the tree, but the Fir Tree did not care.

At Christmastime quite young trees were cut down; trees that were younger and smaller than this impatient Fir Tree. These beautiful young trees did not have their branches chopped off when they were put onto wagons and taken out of the woods.

"Where are they all going?" asked the Fir Tree. "Some are much smaller than me. Why do they keep all their branches? Where are they being taken?"

"We know! We know!" chirped the sparrows. "In the town we are always peeping through the windows, so we know where they go. They get decorated in the most wonderful way you could possibly imagine. We have looked in at the windows and seen them planted in pots in the warm sitting room and covered with the most beautiful things—gilt apples, honey cakes, toys, and hundreds of candles."

"And then?" asked the Fir Tree, trembling through all its branches. "And then? What happens then?"

"Well," said the sparrows, "that's all we saw, but it was wonderful."
"Perhaps that will happen to me one day!" cried the Fir Tree. "That would be even better than traveling across the sea. If only it were Christmas now! Oh, if only I were being carted off! If only I were in the warm sitting room decorated with lovely things. And then? What would happen? It must be something even more wonderful. Why would they decorate me? Oh, I wish this would happen to me!"

"Be happy here with us," said the air and the sunshine. "Be happy here in the woodlands."

But the Fir Tree was not at all happy. It grew and grew and stood there, green, dark green. The people who saw it said, "That's a handsome tree!" and at Christmastime it was cut down before any of the others. The ax cut deep into its trunk, and the tree fell to the ground with a sigh—it felt pain and was now sad at parting from its home. It knew that it would never again see its dear friends, the little bushes and flowers— perhaps not even the birds.

The tree only came to when it was unloaded in a yard with the other trees, and it heard a man say, "This one is the best. We only want this one!"

Now two servants came in bright uniforms and carried the Fir Tree into a large, beautiful room. All around the walls hung pictures, and by the great stove stood huge Chinese vases with lions on them.

There were rocking chairs, silken sofas, tables covered with picture books, and hundreds of toys everywhere.

The Fir Tree was put into a large pot filled with sand. The tree trembled! What would happen next? The servants and the children decorated it. On the branches they hung little bags cut out of colored paper. Each bag was filled with candy; golden apples and walnuts hung down as if they grew there, and hundreds of little candles were fastened to the boughs. Dolls that looked exactly like real people hung from other branches, and right at the very top of the tree a tinsel star was placed. It was magnificent, quite magnificent.

"This evening," said everybody, "this evening the star will shine."

Oh, thought the Fir Tree, *if only it were evening already! Oh, I do hope the candles will soon be lit. I wonder if the trees will come out of the forest to look at me? And will the sparrows peep in at the windows? Will I stay here decorated forever and ever?*

All these questions gave the tree a backache, and a backache is just as bad for a tree as a headache is for a person.

At last the candles were lit. What brilliance, what splendor! The Fir Tree trembled so much that one of the candles set fire to a green twig, but the fire was quickly put out.

And now the doors were opened wide, and the children rushed in. They stared at the tree silently, but only for a minute. They started shouting joyfully and dancing around the tree, pulling at their presents.

What are they doing? thought the Fir Tree. *What's going on?*

The candles burned down, the children pulled the candy off the tree and danced around with their new toys. No one looked at the tree any more except one old man, who came up and peeped among the branches to see if all the nuts and apples had been eaten.

"A story! A story!" shouted the children, and they drew a jolly man toward the tree; and he sat down just beneath it.

"Let's pretend we're in the green woods," he said, "and that the tree can hear my story."

And the jolly man told the story of Klumpey-Dumpey, who was always falling down the stairs and yet in the end married a princess. The Fir Tree stood quite silent and thoughtful; never had the birds in the woods told such a story as that. Klumpey-Dumpey always falling down stairs and yet married a princess!

"Well! Well!" said the Fir Tree. "Who knows? Perhaps I shall fall down the stairs too and marry a princess!" And it looked forward to being decorated again the next evening with candles and toys and fruit.

But in the morning the servants came and dragged it out of the room and upstairs to the attic and put it in a dark corner where no daylight shone. *What's the meaning of this?* thought the tree. *What am I doing here? What's happening?*

And it leaned against the wall and thought and thought. And it had enough time, for days and nights went by, and nobody came up. The tree seemed to be quite forgotten.

Now it's winter outside, said the Fir Tree. The earth is hard and covered with snow, and people cannot plant me. I suppose I'm to be sheltered here until the spring comes. How thoughtful! How good people are! If only it were not so dark here and so lonely. It was pretty out there in the woods, when the snow lay thick and that hare came springing over me; but then I did not like it. It is terribly lonely up here!

Suddenly two little mice crept out. They sniffed at the Fir Tree and then climbed into its branches.

"It's terribly cold up here," said the two little mice. "Don't you think so, old tree?"

"I'm not old," said the Fir Tree.

"Where do you come from?" asked the mice. "And what do you know?" They were very inquisitive. "Tell us about the most beautiful place in the world! Have you been there?"

"The most beautiful place in the world," said the tree, "is the woods, where the sun shines and where the birds sing." And then it told the mice all about its youth.

The little mice listened and said, "What a lot of things you have seen! How happy you must have been!"

"Yes," said the Fir Tree, "those were really quite happy times." But then it told them about the Christmas Eve when it had been decorated with candy and candles.

"Oh!" said the little mice. "How happy you have been, old tree!"

"I'm not old," said the tree. "I only came out of the woods this winter."

"What splendid stories you can tell!" said the little mice.

And the next night they came with four other little mice to hear what the tree had to tell.

So the Fir Tree told them the story of Klumpey-Dumpey, and the little mice ran right to the top of the tree with pleasure. The next night a great many more mice came, and the Fir Tree told the same story again. But when they found out that the tree did not know any other stories, the mice grew bored and went away.

The Fir Tree was sad.

"It was very nice when the merry little mice listened to my story, but it will soon be the spring now. I will be so pleased when they take me out of this lonely place."

When the spring came, people came and rummaged in the attic. A servant dragged the tree downstairs where the daylight shone.

Now life is beginning again! thought the tree.

It felt the fresh air and the sunbeams in the courtyard. The courtyard was close to a garden where the roses were in flower, the trees were in full leaf, and the swallows were singing.

"Now I will live!" said the tree joyfully and spread its branches out; but alas! They were all withered and yellow; it lay in the corner among nettles and weeds. The tinsel star was still on it and shone in the bright sunshine.

In the courtyard the children who had danced around the tree at Christmas were playing. One of them ran up and tore off the golden star. "Look what is sticking to the ugly old fir tree," said the child, and he stepped on the branches until they cracked under his boots.

And the tree looked at all the flowers and the lovely garden and then looked at itself and wished it had stayed in the dark corner of the attic. It thought of its fresh youth in the woods, of the merry Christmas Eve, and of the little mice who had listened so happily to the story of Klumpey-Dumpey.

"Past! Past!" said the old tree. "It's all over. If only I had been happier at the time."

And a servant came and chopped the tree into little pieces; a whole bundle lay there. It blazed brightly in the stove, and it sighed deeply, and each sigh was like a little explosion. The children sat down by the fire, looked into it, and cried, "Snap! Crackle!"

But at each explosion, which was a deep sigh, the tree thought of a summer day in the woods or of a winter night there when the stars shone. It thought of Christmas Eve and of Klumpey-Dumpey, the only story it had ever heard or knew how to tell; and then the tree was burned.

The children played in the garden, and the youngest put on the golden star that the tree had worn on its happiest evening.

Now that was over, and the tree's life was over, and the story is over, too!

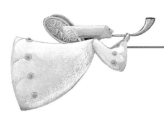

Notes on the Authors

Anne Adeney has written more than 20 books for children—her favorite of which is *The Biggest Bible Storybook* (2003). Previously she was a housemother to Inuit children in northern Canada and then worked as an occupational therapist specializing in psychiatry and designed and made award-winning wooden toys. She lives in Devon, England, with her husband and four children.

Louisa May Alcott (1832–1888) was born in Pennsylvania. She worked as a teacher, seamstress, domestic servant, and as an army nurse during the U.S. Civil War. She also edited a children's magazine, *Merry's Museum*, in which the story "Becky's Christmas Dream" was first published. Her most famous novel, *Little Women*, was published in 1868.

Hans Christian Andersen (1805–1875) was born in Odense, Denmark. His family was very poor, and he received little early education. He worked as a tailor, a weaver, and an actor before returning to school at the age of 17. He eventually went to Copenhagen University and began a career as a writer—producing plays, travel books, and novels. He is best known for his fairy tales and stories, including "The Fir Tree," which was written in 1844.

Antonia Barber grew up with ballet. Her father worked at the Royal Opera House

in London, England, where she met many great performers, including her favorite dancer, Margot Fonteyn. She has written many books for children, including *The Mousehole Cat*, winner of the Children's Book Award and now a popular movie. Antonia lives in England.

Nora Clarke was born in Yorkshire, England. She worked as a teacher in Hong Kong and then in the publishing industry when she returned to England. She began writing new versions of old legends and original stories for children when her own children were young and has contributed to several Kingfisher anthologies of stories. She lives in Gloucestershire, England, with her husband.

Charles Dickens (1812–1870) was born in Portsmouth, England. When he was only twelve years old, his father was sent to prison for debt, and Charles himself went to work in a factory. With great determination he became a shorthand reporter in the House of Commons and went on to write the novels that would make him incredibly popular. *A Christmas Carol* was published on December 17, 1843. The novel sold an impressive 6,000 copies by Christmas Eve.

Vivian French trained as an actress and storyteller and has a passion for sharing

her tales aloud. She has been nominated for many awards, including the Smarties Prize in the U.K. with *A Song for Toad*. She lives in Edinburgh, Scotland, but she regularly visits schools throughout the U.K. and tours often.

Kenneth Grahame (1859–1932) was born in Edinburgh, Scotland, but following the death of his mother he was sent to live with his grandmother in Berkshire, England, where he grew up. He worked in the Bank of England for many years, writing essays and stories in his spare time. He created the characters in *The Wind in the Willows* while writing letters to his son, Alastair. The book was published in 1908.

The Brothers Grimm, Jacob (1785–1863) and Wilhelm (1786–1859), were born in Hanau, Germany. In 1806, after studying law at the University of Marburg, they began to collect folktales from Germany and beyond. They devoted their lives to this work, producing many books and articles on linguistics, folklore, and medieval studies and were celebrated by scholars and readers alike.

William Dean Howells (1837–1920) was born in Ohio. His education consisted of reading a lot while helping his father, who worked as a printer. Howells became a writer, producing a biography of Abraham Lincoln and some travel books. His novels— noted for their realism—achieved huge popularity, and as a critic he promoted the work of Mark Twain and Stephen Crane, among others.

Lucy Maud (L. M.) Montgomery (1874–1942) was born on Prince Edward Island, off the coast of Canada. She first became a schoolteacher, then a postmistress, and also worked as a journalist before beginning her career as a novelist. She was the author of many novels for children, most notably *Anne of Green Gables*, published in 1908. This was the first of eight books featuring the lively, redheaded heroine; they are still popular today. L. M. Montgomery also wrote hundreds of short stories.

Ann Pilling was born in 1944 and educated in Lancashire, England, where many of her books are set. She studied english at London University, taught for awhile, and became a full-time writer in 1979. Her 11 books for children include the award-winning novel *Henry's Leg*. She is married with two sons and lives in Oxford, England.

Saviour Pirotta has written more than 60 children's fiction and information books that have been translated into ten languages. He has a special interest in myths and traditional legends from around the world. Saviour was born in Malta and is a trained chef. He lives in Brighton, England.

Fiona Waters has spent all her working life with children's books. She has been a bookseller and editor, and she now runs a book club, working closely with U.K. schools and libraries. She is a consultant, a reviewer, and a compiler of several anthologies, including three Kingfisher treasuries. She lives in Dorset, England.

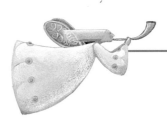

Acknowledgments

The publisher would like to thank the copyright holders for permission to reproduce the following copyright material:

"The First Christmas" by **Anne Adeney** copyright © Anne Adeney 2004; "The Nutcracker" taken from *Tales from the Ballet* by **Antonia Barber** (Kingfisher 1995) copyright © Antonia Barber 1995; "A Very Big Cat" by **Nora Clarke** taken from *A Treasury of Christmas Stories* (Kingfisher) copyright © Kingfisher 1985; "Befana and the Three Wise Men" by **Vivian French** copyright © Vivian French 2004; "The Fir Tree" taken from *A Treasury of Stories from Hans Christian Andersen* retold by **Jenny Koralek** (Kingfisher 1996) copyright © Jenny Koralek 1996; "Aunt Cyrilla's Christmas Basket" taken from *Christmas with Anne* by **Lucy Maud Montgomery**. Used by permission, McClelland & Stewart Ltd. The Canadian Publishers. L. M. Montgomery is a trademark of the Heirs of L. M. Montgomery, Inc.; "The Legend of St. Nicholas" by **Ann Pilling** copyright © Ann Pilling 2004; "A Gift from the Heart" by **Saviour Pirotta** copyright © Saviour Pirotta 2004; "Old Pierre's Christmas Visitors" by **Fiona Waters** copyright © Fiona Waters 2004.

Every effort has been made to obtain permission to reproduce copyright material but there may be cases where we have been unable to trace a copyright holder. The publisher will be happy to correct any omissions in future printings.

The publishers would like to thank the artists for their illustrations as follows:

Illustrations for "Becky's Christmas" copyright © **Greg Becker** 2004; Illustrations for "The Elves and the Shoemaker" copyright © **Helen Cann** 2004; Illustrations for "Befana and the Three Wise Men" copyright © **Paolo D'Altan** 2004; Illustrations for "Christmas Every Day" copyright © **Alastair Graham** 2004; Illustrations for "The Cratchits' Christmas Dinner" copyright © **Susan Hellard** 2004; Illustrations for "A Gift from the Heart" copyright © **Claire Henley** 2004; Illustrations for "Old Pierre's Christmas Visitors" copyright © **Paul Hess** 2004; Illustrations for "Aunt Cyrilla's Christmas Basket" © 2004 **Suzanna Hubbard**; Illustrations for "The Fir Tree" copyright © **Martin Irish** 2004; Illustrations for "The First Christmas" copyright © **Richard Johnson** 2004; Illustrations for "A Very Big Cat" copyright © **Anna C. Leplar** 2004; Illustrations for "Christmas at Mole End" copyright © **Georgina McBain** 2004; Illustrations for "The Nutcracker" copyright © **Olywn Whelan** 2004; Illustrations for "The Legend of St. Nicholas" copyright © **Sharon Williams** 2004.